Discarded

THE ORIGIN AND EVOLUTION
OF OUR OWN PARTICULAR UNIVERSE

Books by David E. Fisher

NOVELS

Crisis
Compartments
A Fearful Symmetry
The Last Flying Tiger
The Man You Sleep With
Variation on a Theme
Katie's Terror
Grace for the Dead

SCIENCE AND HISTORY

Creation of the Universe
Creation of Atoms and Stars
The Ideas of Einstein
The Third Experiment
The Birth of the Earth
A Dance on the Edge of Time
The Origin and Evolution of Our Own Particular Universe

THE ORIGIN
AND EVOLUTION
OF OUR OWN
PARTICULAR
UNIVERSE

by David E. Fisher

Illustrated with diagrams and photographs

ATHENEUM   1988   NEW YORK

The photograph of the Crab Nebula on page 90 courtesy of Palomar Observatory.

Atheneum
Macmillan Publishing Company
866 Third Avenue, New York, NY 10022
Collier Macmillan Canada, Inc.
First Edition   Designed by Eliza Green
Printed in the United States of America

10   9   8   7   6   5   4   3   2   1

Library of Congress Cataloging-in-Publication Data
Fisher, David E.
The origin and evolution of our own particular universe
David E. Fisher.—1st ed.   p.   cm.   Bibliography: p. 169 Includes index.
Summary: Presents known facts and theories on the beginnings of our universe and its evolution over millions of years.
ISBN 0–689–31368–3
1. Cosmology—Juvenile literature. 2. Astronomy—Juvenile literature. [1. Cosmology. 2. Astronomy.] I. Title.
QB983.F57   1988   523.1—dc19   88–14108 CIP AC

*An unknown "man from Mexico named
Jorge," upon paying twenty-five cents to
a street astronomer to look through a
telescope at Jupiter and the stars:
"I look at the sky and I feel better. I see
one star, and I look at the world different."
—quoted by Judith Stone,
in* Moonlighting
(Discover, October 1987)

To Jorge, and to Tony Hoffman,
the New York street astronomer,
this book is gratefully dedicated

CONTENTS

PART THREE: THE EARTH

PART FOUR: PAST AND FUTURE WORLDS

Introduction

How do we begin a book like this?

There are two possible ways. We could begin with the smallest and build up to the biggest: start with the creation of life, then the creation of this planet we live on, then the solar system, and finally the stars to complete the universe. Or we could do the opposite, beginning with the creation of the universe and getting progressively smaller from there to the creation of stars and the sun, the earth, and finally ourselves.

If we follow the advice of the queen to Alice, we shall start at the beginning, and that means the second alternative, for the universe came first and our planet and ourselves came last.

And that is a remarkable thing to say. Because how do we know? If we were gods and wanted to create a universe, wouldn't it seem easier to build a small planet first and then build more planets and then a sun to give it light and then lots of stars—the way you and I build anything: begin with the simplest part and then add onto it. But that's not the way it happened.

How do we know that's not the way it happened? How can we *know* how it all was created? That's the most intriguing question of all, and it's the heart of this book. . . .

PART I

THE BEGINNING

ONE

The Greek World

1. IN ORDER TO UNDERSTAND SOMETHING, WE MUST first know what it is; only then can we begin to think about *why* it is and how it got to be that way. And so with the universe we must first know what it is we are talking about, what it looks like, what it is composed of.

There are two ways to describe the universe. One is in terms of its parts, what it is composed of, its atoms and stars and planets. The other is in terms of the principles that guide it. Underlying both these descriptions must always be the question: How do you know? How do you *know* the universe you are describing is actually composed of these precise stars and planets and no others, how do you know there aren't other *things* out there forever unsuspected, and how do you know the principles we talk about are the true principles underlying our universe?

The answer is that we don't know everything there is to be known, but we do know an awful lot. The best way to get an understanding of the extent of our present knowledge—almost all of which has come only within our present century—is to start with the first beginnings of mankind's quest to understand this universe, to see how we have tried and where we have made mistakes, and why we think we are finally on the right track.

2. The first attempts to understand the universe were in terms of magic, poetry, and mythology, and unfortunately they didn't work. Why "unfortunately"? Because it would be fun to live in such a universe, with stars pulled across the heavens by dragons or angels, with gods throwing thunderbolts from clouds or mountaintops, with beautiful goddesses stepping forth from seashells and falling in love with heroes and war-

3

riors. And why do I say that such a universe doesn't work? Because the predictions based on such a model didn't come true: Praying to the gods for rich harvests or good weather didn't produce any better result than ignoring them did; throwing teenage girls into boiling volcanoes didn't stop the eruptions; cutting open the guts of chickens and staring into the spilled entrails didn't predict the future; and studying the positions the stars were in when you were born didn't tell you anything at all about what fate held in store.

But, at least in the last example, it led to something better. The ancient Egyptians found that while the stars didn't control people's destinies, they did control—or at least predict—the seasons. And that, for the Egyptians, was quite literally a matter of life and death, of extinction or survival.

Egypt is a raw and barren desert, except for the life-giving waters of the Nile, which since the beginnings of time have flowed mysteriously from the sun-baked southern deserts—where no water ought to flow— to irrigate the Nile Valley and make Egypt one of the most fertile of the ancient kingdoms. The source of the Nile was hidden beyond the impenetrable desert, so no one knew whence it came, and its action was like magic: Each year, at the peak of the hot, dry, summer season, when it seemed as if all the world must dry up and die under the terrible sun, the waters of the Nile would suddenly begin to swell and flow with a majestic power, finally overflowing their banks and spilling out in luxurious wetness over the land, flooding it and soaking it with life-sustaining water. When the floods receded again, the dusty land on either side was dusty no longer but once again became fertile and ripe for planting.

If ever a year passed when the Nile waters did not flood, people died of famine. And so each summer the high priests led the people in prayers and supplication—and each year the prayers of the priests were answered. In gratitude the people rewarded them with honor, prestige, and power—for surely these priests understood and could influence the will of the gods.

Hardly. What those priests understood was that when the sun and the star Sirius rose together in the morning sky, it meant that the Nile would soon overflow. And so each night they watched the rising and setting of Sirius, waiting for it to begin to match that of the sun, and as the motions of the star and the sun came closer, they would begin to call the people together for their annual prayer. Carefully gauging Sirius's progression, they would reach a climax of prayer just as it matched the sun, movement for movement, and when the Nile then flowed over its banks, they would reap the thanks of the populace.

Knowledge is power. We have seen that demonstrated most awfully to us in this century, over Hiroshima and Nagasaki, and it was just as true then.

The Egyptian priests in those ancient days didn't understand what they were seeing; they didn't know what the Sirius-sun conjunction could have to do with the Nile; they simply knew that it worked. Over the next two thousand years they, and the Greek civilization that succeeded them, studied in more detail the workings of the heavens and their relations with the earth.

By the sixth century B.C. a group of Greek scholars called the Pythagoreans, after their leader, had a reasonable understanding of the universe. They observed that the sun rose every day in the east and settled in the west: While earlier people had believed that the god Helios formed the sun in his eastern workshop every morning and then propelled it across the sky in his chariot, finally sinking it into the western ocean every evening, the Pythagoreans worked out a more rational explanation. If the earth were the center of the universe and the sun simply moved around it in a circle, that would explain the observations without recourse to such beings as gods, which, after all, had never been seen. But why should the sun move around the earth in a circle?

And here we come to the other way of describing the universe— according to the principles on which it is founded. It began when the Greeks noticed something funny about the universe: the different ways things move or don't move. A man standing alone in the middle of a field doesn't move unless he wants to. That is, he feels nothing pushing him to the left or the right or up or down; he simply stands there. So does a stone, or a piece of wood. Put them down on the ground, and they don't bounce around; they simply lie still. So a basic principle might be that objects in the universe tend to be still.

But then imagine a man climbing a tree and then stepping gently off the branch into thin air: He doesn't stand still then, does he? He falls down. And so do other objects. A stone thrown into the air doesn't keep on rising, nor does it reach a certain height and then stop. It falls back down again. So the basic principle seemed to be that objects tend to fall down to the ground.

But this was not a satisfactory principle, for what great significance can the ground have? It bothered the Greeks that the dirt under their feet should be so important that it pulled everything to it, and then they came up with a great insight. It wasn't the ground that was important; it was the center of the universe that was! They envisaged the earth as a great ball, and the center of the earth was the center of the universe, and all things would "naturally" fall toward that center. The only significance of the ground was that it broke the fall and prevented further motion toward the center.

This seemed to be a principle of great significance, but again there was a problem: The sun and the moon and the stars don't fall down. Why not?

The Greeks came up with a second great principle: On earth all natural motion is down, toward the center of the universe, which is why people fall down from mountains instead of falling up or sideways. But the heavens, in contrast to our pitiful earth, are perfect and everlasting—and so the only motion permissible to them is that most perfect of all motions, circular. The circle, according to the reasoning of the Greeks, is the most perfect geometrical figure, without beginning or end or changes along its length. Therefore, the sun must move in a circle around the center of the universe instead of plunging down toward it, as things on earth are constrained to do.

The stars, too, should move in this heavenly circle, they reasoned, and indeed they do. When the Greeks stood on their mountaintops and watched the stars, they saw them rise in the east and descend in the west, just as the sun does. And so their observations of the universe and their principles of the universe fit together to give an understandable picture, or model, of what the universe really is.

They learned a lot more about the universe. About 300 B.C., Euclid formulated his famous rules of geometry, one of which stated that the sum of the angles of a triangle always is equal to exactly 180 degrees. But the Egyptian farmers, while laying out triangular plots of land for farming, had noticed centuries before that the sum of the angles included in their triangles was *greater* than 180 degrees. Mathematicians now realized that this could be true if the triangles were laid out on a curved surface instead of a flat one.

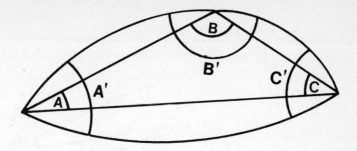

Each of the curved angles A', B', C', is greater than the corresponding flat angles A, B, C, and so their sum must be greater. Since the triangles concerned were those laid out on the surface of the earth, the Greeks learned in this way that the surface of the earth is curved, not flat. A hundred years later Eratosthenes realized that when he had lived in Cyene, in southern Egypt, the sun was directly overhead at noon every year on June 21, but when he moved three hundred miles north to Alexandria this was no longer true. He reasoned that this, too, was due to the curvature of the earth and in fact was able to use Euclid's geometry to calculate the curvature. He deduced a value for the radius of the earth in excellent agreement with what we know it to be today.

The Greek concept of the universe was a particularly satisfying one; it must have been, for it lasted two thousand years before it was seriously challenged. There were minor objections along the way, of course. Sometime around 270 B.C. Aristarchus of Samos suggested that it was the sun that was actually at the universe's center rather than the earth, but nobody paid much attention. There was no reason to; the Greek universe was perfect.

3. Well, not quite. There was one problem: the planets. These were "stars" (or so they seemed to be) that didn't follow the perfect circular motion of the sun and all the other stars but instead moved in peculiar back-and-forth motions across the night skies. During any one night the planets looked like normal stars, but whereas the stars kept their positions relative to each other firmly from one night to the other—so that groups of stars could be imagined to form objects in the sky, like the Big and Little Dippers—the planets moved with respect to the "fixed" stars and in a meandering sort of way.

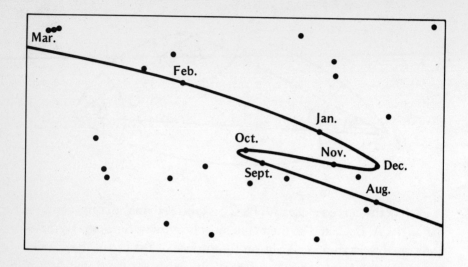

This didn't fit the principle that the heavenly bodies moved only in circular paths. The Greek philosopher Plato was the first person we know of to point out this problem, which was "solved" by his pupil Eudoxus of Cnidus in the fourth century B.C., when he postulated a model in which the planets moved in circles upon circles. To understand this, imagine a bicycle wheel with a smaller wheel pinned to its rim. The heavenly wheels are invisible, Eudoxus suggested, and the planets are pinned to the rim of the smaller wheel. Then, as both wheels revolve, the planets show a reversible motion.

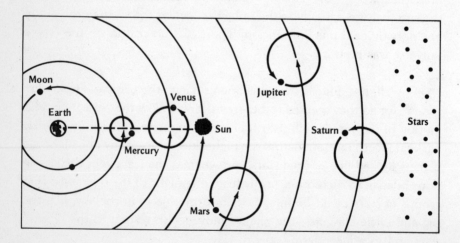

In the succeeding centuries, as the motions of the planets were measured more and more accurately, discrepancies were found between their observed motions and those predicted by this wheels-upon-wheels model. But each time a correction was needed, it was possible to provide it by simply adding another wheel to the universal scheme so that the planets were imagined to move on wheels-upon-wheels-upon-wheels-upon . . .

And this brings us to a new concept.

4. When the Greeks postulated that "natural" motion was in a downward direction on earth but circular in the heavens, they didn't offer any explanation of why this might be so. They simply observed that this was the way things were. Looking back from the vantage of our own time, we can suggest two basic principles that might lead to it. One is the principle of beauty, the other of simplicity.

The latter was put forth in the fourteenth century by an English philosopher, William of Occam, and has come to be known as Occam's Razor; it is often stated as "Entities should not be multiplied unnecessarily." That is, the simplest solution to a problem often turns out to be the right one. In order to solve a problem, one should try to think of the simplest solution. If it turns out—as one learns more about the original problem—that the simple solution requires a lot of fiddling around with the original concept, if entities are being multiplied and simplicity is being lost, then one should begin to think about throwing away the original attempt and beginning over again.

The other principle, that of beauty, is one that has become popular only in the present century. Somehow it seems that the universe is put together with an eye for beauty, or perhaps this is only a reflection of the other principle, beauty and simplicity often being related.

These principles are vague and hard to follow. For example, Einstein's equations of gravity are more complicated than Newton's, and yet they are more correct; so simplicity does not always win. But other theories have been proposed to explain the same facts that Einstein's do; they are more complicated still, and they have turned out to be wrong.

Beauty is even harder to define. Which is more beautiful, Beethoven's string quartets or Bruce Springsteen's songs? The answer is obvious, but how do you convince people who disagree?

Still, with all these difficulties, beauty and simplicity are useful if rough guidelines to the truth. If we accept them, we can see how the early Greek ideas of two natural motions—one for the earth and the other for the heavens—fit these basic principles and therefore might well be the truth upon which the universe is constructed.

But then, as the world trudged wearily through nearly twenty centuries of Greek science and philosophy, the added circles-upon-circles, which became necessary in order to describe the motions of the planets, began to seem to some people less and less simple, less and less beautiful.

Something new was needed.

TWO
Copernicus

1.   THE GREEK UNIVERSE NEVER LED TO ANY PICTURE of its origin. It was too perfect, with everything moving around in circles; it seemed as if it must always have existed, and so neither in mythology nor in science nor philosophy did the Greeks ever seriously question or discuss its origin.

The Copernican universe is something else again.

2.   Nicolaus Copernicus, the son of a Polish trader, was born in the fifteenth century. Europe at that time was emerging from the Dark Ages, a period of intellectual desolation when political chaos combined with a domineering and dogmatic church to stifle not only dissent from established views but also the very possibility of original thought and inquiry. As Europe slowly awoke from its long sleep, here and there a few individuals popped up who began again the slow quest for knowledge.

Scholars did not specialize in those days. Physicians did not split into internists and orthopedists and heart and gastrointestinal specialists. There were no physicists or chemists, no metallurgists or engineers; there were simply scholars. This is not because people were wiser in those times, but rather the opposite: There was not enough known in any one discipline to constitute a body of knowledge large enough to occupy a man.

And so the boy Copernicus studied everything and became, as he grew up, a mathematician and an artist, a doctor and a priest, an astronomer and an economist. In 1501 he became canon of the cathedral of Frauenburg, later served as physician to the bishop of Ermeland, and in 1522 he devised a scheme for reforming the Polish currency. And

11

wherever he traveled throughout Europe he warmly and eagerly discussed with his few intellectual friends the absorbing questions of the day, chief among which was the structure of the universe.

The observed motions of the sun and the stars could most simply and beautifully be explained if they circled the earth. But those damned planets complicated the scheme terribly. By this time so many circles upon circles had been found to be necessary—if their proposed motions were to agree with the observations—that some people were beginning to wonder if there mightn't be a different and simpler scheme.

And so they began to wonder if perhaps the earth were one of the planets. Because if it were, and if it traveled around the sun along with the other planets, the *observed* planetary motions might not be *true* motions at all.

We are all familiar with the fact that if we view something from a moving source, the thing viewed appears to be in motion. If you are sitting in a train as it pulls out of the station, or in a jet as it leaves the terminal, as you glance out the window your first impression is that it is the station or the terminal that is moving. If you are in a car traveling at fifty miles an hour and pass a car going at forty, and if you look at the other car and not at the passing scenery, you have the impression that the other car is moving backward as you pass it.

Now you know that the station and the terminal are not really moving[1] and that the other car is not really driving backward along the interstate highway, but if you weren't convinced that such motion is impossible, and if you weren't aware of your own motion, you would certainly think that they were.

Suppose, Copernicus's young friends argued, that the earth is in motion around the sun and we don't know it. Then what would the motion of the planets look like to us? They would certainly change their positions, as we see them, relative to the fixed stars (which were assumed to be stationary, or fixed, in space far beyond the planets). The planets would even seem to move backward if we were moving faster and passed them in our race around the sun. As Copernicus's friends worked out the details, it looked very much as if the apparent motion of the planets

[1]This is not strictly true. We'll come back to discuss it when we get to Einstein's theory of relativity.

as viewed from a moving earth would match quite closely their actual motions that we observed. The "modern" European model would look like this:

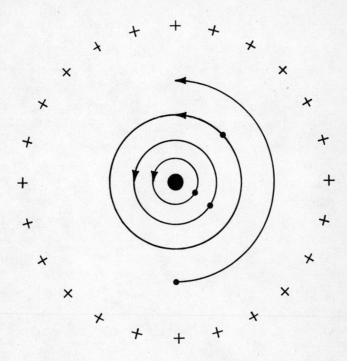

Obviously this newer scheme (which has since become known as the Copernican system; though Copernicus did not originate it, the book that he wrote popularized it and spread its message throughout Europe and the world) is simpler. Actually, the improved simplicity of this model may not be readily apparent from the diagram, for the Greek model, on page 8, has itself been simplified in order to render it readable; if you will imagine each planet moving in a series of circles upon circles instead of in the simple circle on a circle shown, its complexity will be revealed. The Copernican model, on the other hand, shows simply each planet moving in a circle around the sun, the moon moving in a circle around the earth, and the stars fixed far away in space. What could be simpler?

Nicolaus Copernicus

As for beauty, it is of course in the eye of the beholder, but aren't the stark and simple lines of the Copernican model more lovely to contemplate than the tortured circularities of the old Greeks?

There were, however, stronger lines of argument than beauty and simplicity to be pursued in the name of Truth. What about, people said, the Word of God?

3. What about it, indeed?

Well, we had the Bible, didn't we? And it told us all we needed to know about the universe and its creation, didn't it? In particular it told us (*Genesis* 1:18) that "God set them [the sun and moon] in the heavens to shine on the earth, to govern the day and the night and to divide light from darkness." This makes no direct statement about which is the center, but it certainly makes an implication: If the sun was created for the express purpose of shining on the earth, then the earth is certainly the more important of the two—it is, after all, the reason the other was created. And since all creation in the Bible leads up to *us* as the culmination of the Creator's grand design and the earth is our home, it surely follows that the earth is the important body and the sun is secondary. And therefore the earth must have the most important place in the universe instead of simply circling with all the other planets around the great center.

In Copernicus's time there was no great confrontation between the Church and those who followed his reasoning, but in the century that followed, the Church leaders began to worry about the consequences of allowing free thought about so fundamental a question. One extremist on the Copernican side, Giordano Bruno, went so far as to suggest that the other planets were in all respects similar to the earth, they were worlds in their own right, and if that were true they might even have people living on them. But if *that* were true, it would have terrible implications for the idea that we here on earth were God's chosen people (an idea the Church took, along with so much more, from the ancient Hebrews). It all began to smack of heresy.

And so the Inquisition stepped in, and Giordano Bruno was burned alive at the stake.[2]

But you might as well emulate poor old King Canute, and stand on the seashore and command the tides not to come in as stand in the pulpit and command people not to think. (Most of the ocean, of course, does *not* come in; only an infinitesimal portion crosses the low-tide mark on the beach and soaks the sands. Most of the ocean remains in its wet abyss obeying the king. And most of the people will gladly not bother to think . . . but *some* will, and like the small, stubborn ocean waters that cross the sands, nothing will stop them.)

Copernicus died in bed, and Bruno died at the stake, but their ideas were made of hardier stuff.

[2]To save his soul, of course. Isn't civilization wonderful?

THREE
The First Scientists

I. AND HERE WE COME TO THE CRUX OF THIS BOOK, which is not only about the universe but also about *us.* One question that we want to answer is how our universe was created, but the other question, perhaps even more important, is how we learned the answer.

Because here we are, alone and on our own, strangers in a strange land, standing on this whirling earth as it caroms through the galaxy, looking out at the sun and the stars, wondering what's really out there and where it came from, wondering who we really are and where we came from—and there's nobody in the universe to tell us. We have to dig out the answers for ourselves.

And the answers don't come wrapped in a blue ribbon with a tag that says, "Congratulations, you're right!" They come, when they come at all, slithering in through cracks and crevices, often unnoticed and un-recognized. So the most important question is, How do we learn? How do we know if we have the right answer or the wrong? How do we know when we're on the right track, or when we're out in left field?

We can look for simplicity and beauty in our answers, but we can't rely on them as guides, as we're about to find out in the case of the Copernican universe.

What we *can* rely on is the concept of testability. In the days of Copernicus this was a new and radical doctrine. What people had relied on since time immemorial was an appeal to authority. When they had a problem, they would go to their rabbi to hear what the Torah said or to their bishop to hear what Thomas Aquinas said or to the ancient Greek texts to find out what Aristotle said. Copernicus himself was a traditionalist in this regard; he wrote that "we must agree to follow

16

strictly the methods of the ancients and to keep to their observations, which we regard as a holy Testament. To those unwilling to trust the ancients implicitly, the doors of my science must be closed."

In writing those words, he showed himself to be no true scientist at all. For the basis of science is to trust no one and nothing that is not tested. The story is told of the group of ancient philosophers who sat around all night, arguing about how many teeth were in the mouth of a horse. One young apprentice stood up and suggested that they simply step outside into the barn and *look*. They strung him up by his thumbs and went happily on with their discussion.

They weren't stupid; they were simply more interested in the *concept* of a horse, and in how many teeth it *should* have compared with other animals that were more or less similar or different. The apprentice missed the point; he was the first scientist—the man who is interested in what *is* rather than in what *might be* or *should be*.

Science is nothing holy, nothing angelic or godlike. There are many other philosophies that a person might with confidence follow in this world; there are many other paths that a person might take for the ultimate good of all. We're glad that Beethoven was a musician and Noel Coward a playwright, that Renoir became an artist and Rodin a sculptor and Tolstoy a novelist; these men were not scientists, knew nothing of the workings of science, and they have produced works of beauty that have enriched millions of lives. Science is not all, not everything, but it is quite simply and quite indisputably the best path to truth, the best way to find out about the material universe in which we live.

The basis of this method of truth finding that we call science is the concept of testability. Any idea or model or view of the universe or of any small part of the universe must be tested by comparing what it says to what we actually *see*, and by "see" I include methods beyond that in which we use our own eyes: We can see through microscopes and telescopes and through more complicated instruments, such as mass spectrometers and CAT scans and magnetic imagers, and the like. We can measure things and compare the results with our theory and in this way test whether or not we are on the right track.

That's how we found out which theory about the universe was right, the Greek or the Copernican. Two men, perhaps the first two real scientists of any importance in the history of the world, set out to test the two theories—and found that neither theory was right.

3. The most impressive thing about Tycho Brahe's appearance was his nose. The original one, which God had given him, he left behind early one morning in a forest clearing in Denmark, sliced off in a sword duel. He replaced it, on formal occasions, with a nose made of gold and silver.

The most impressive thing about his mind was his insistence on finding the answer to the age-old riddle of the structure of the universe by comparing the two major theories with observation. But at that time, toward the end of the sixteenth century, some thirty years after Copernicus's death, the observations simply weren't good enough. Either theory could account for them, within the rather large limits of error.

Error is an intrinsic part of any measurement; it cannot be avoided, at least in any complex situation. You might be able to count a half-dozen apples without making an error, but in no way could you count the grains of sand on the beaches of the world without making a mistake. The important thing in science is to estimate the precision of the measurement, which means estimating the error involved.

Brahe devoted the rest of his life to making astronomical measurements more and more precise, with the ultimate object in mind of testing the astronomical theories. He had actually a third theory of his own. He rejected the Greek theory because it was too cluttered with circles, and he rejected the Copernican theory for two even better reasons. The first one was that Copernicus had stated that the earth was in motion around the sun, and it was perfectly clear to him and to everyone else that you couldn't *feel* the earth moving.

In his lifetime, if a person was in motion—on a horse or a boat or falling off a cliff—he *knew* he was moving; he could feel it. Today, with the experience of flying in a jet at 600 miles an hour so smoothly that if we close our eyes we can't tell that we're moving, we realize that it is not motion that can be felt but acceleration.

Acceleration is a shift in motion, a change of either speed or direction, and that is what we feel as we bounce up and down on a horse or a boat or fall from a cliff. (Actually, as the earth revolves around the sun, it is continually changing direction and therefore accelerating, but this acceleration is so slow and so smooth compared with our everyday motions and lives that we can't feel it; our bodies just aren't sensitive enough.)

But in the sixteenth century when a person was in motion, he certainly could feel it, and so Brahe's first objection to the Copernican system was a reasonable one.

His second objection was even stronger: He could prove with mathematics that Copernicus was wrong! To understand his argument, let's consider the following *gedankenexperiment*:[1]

You are standing in front of your house, and there is a tree directly across the street. Now you turn right and walk to the end of the block. Will the tree still be directly across the street from you? Obviously not; it will now be to your left.

Now consider that you are looking up at a particular star on a December night. The star is directly overhead. If the earth is moving around the sun, the star must lie in a different direction when the earth has moved halfway around its path, just as the tree in front of you was no longer in front of you when you walked to the end of the block.

Brahe made many such observations of particular stars, separated by six-month time periods, and found that he could find no such "movement" of the stars. Therefore he concluded that he had proved that the earth does not move.[2]

But despite the fact that he felt the Copernican theory was wrong, he wasn't ready to throw it away. Instead he wanted to test it even more strongly, together with the Greek theory and one of his own. Not accepting either of the other two, he had devised his own picture of the universe. According to him, the planets revolved around the sun, which in turn revolved around the earth. This made sense to him, but making sense isn't enough: He wanted to know if it was true. (Making sense meant that it was possible, but not necessarily true.)

The only way to test the theories was to improve the precision of the experimental numbers, because in Brahe's time each of the theories could account for the positions of the planets as observed from earth, within the limits of error of the previous observations. Brahe was confi-

[1]This is a German word meaning "thought-experiment." It refers to a procedure in which it is sometimes possible to "perform" an experiment simply by thinking about it, and imagining what the results must be.
[2]This is a strong proof, but it has a weakness and in fact is totally wrong. It fails because the stars are much farther away than Brahe imagined. (Perform the tree experiment again, but do it with the moon. Does it "move" as the tree did? Why not?)

dent that if he could measure the positions of the planets more and more accurately, eventually he would find that two of the theories would drop out: They would predict planetary positions in conflict with the more precise data. He reasoned that if only one of the theories was correct, then the other two must be wrong; and if they were wrong, they couldn't possibly give the right positions of the planets. All he had to do was measure their positions accurately enough to distinguish between the correct theory and the incorrect ones.

Sounds easy, but it took years of hard work. It took the rest of his life and a little bit more. Which was a good thing, in a way, because when the results were in, his own theory was proved wrong, and so were the other two.

4. The proving was a difficult matter. Aside from the difficulties in providing sufficiently accurate observations of the planetary positions, someone had to calculate from the theories just where each planet would appear to be on each night, as viewed from earth. To do this supremely difficult and—in those noncomputer days—supremely repetitious and boring task, Brahe hired a young Dutch theological student.

That might seem a curious choice, but remember that in those days scholars didn't specialize. Although Johannes Kepler was indeed a theologian, he was also a mathematician and astronomer. (He also believed in astrology, that ignorant perversion of astronomy, and in spiritualism and metaphysics. He came by these traits naturally: His mother was once arrested as a witch and nearly burned.) But he came to believe in Brahe's idea that the only way to discover the truth was to compare ideas with observations, and so he spent many years in calculating from the theories precisely where each planet must be each night of the year, while Brahe spent his nights observing the planets and plotting their positions.

Kepler "believed" that the Copernican system was the correct one. That was the one he was betting on, but as a scientist he wouldn't really believe it to be true until it confirmed the observations, and the other theories failed to do so. The problem was that all three theories could be made to predict planetary positions that were nearly identical, the difference between them being so small as to be—by the methods available at that time—nearly immeasurable. Still Brahe did not despair, and when he died in 1601 he left behind a host of detailed observations that

Johannes Kepler

took years to turn into the proper form for comparison with the theories.

When Kepler eventually managed to do this, he found that Brahe's theory was quite definitely wrong: The calculations were not in agreement with Brahe's own observations. And so, too, was the Greek theory wrong: Even with the addition of circles upon circles, Kepler was able to show that the theory could not match the precise observations.

Which left only the Copernican theory, to Kepler's great joy (since that was the one he had always championed). But to his distress he now found that one planet, Mars, did not fit that theory either.

Again and again he went over his calculations, until he was sure that there could be no mistake. The precision of Brahe's observations was so impressive that this conclusion was inescapable: The Copernican theory was better than the other two, but it wasn't good enough. It, too, was wrong.

5. And so it was back to the ledgers, with their long columns of numbers, pages and pages of carefully gathered numbers, in a torturous attempt to gather some meaning from them. There had to be an answer: The universe exists, and there *must* be a theory that would explain it.

There was, but it took an act of almost superhuman courage to find the clue. One night, almost in desperation after having tried every trick he could think of, Kepler threw away the circle.

Each of the theories, remember, had been based upon this most perfect of geometric shapes, for in a universe created by an omnipotent God, what other shape would do?[3] And yet, as it turned out, the circle was the barrier that had kept the truth hidden.

Instead of a circle for the orbit of Mars, Kepler tried an ellipse. An ellipse is simply an imperfect circle, or, more accurately, a circle is a particular kind of ellipse. A circle can be drawn by taking a paper and pencil, a tack, and a closed loop of string. Put the tack into the paper and loop the string over it. Then insert the pencil into the loop of string, pull it as far from the tack as it will go, and move it across the paper, keeping the string taut. You will trace out a circle.

For an ellipse simply use two tacks. Put them into the paper, separated by an inch or two, and repeat the experiment. The figure drawn will be an ellipse.

In the circle the single tack is at the *center*. In the ellipse the two tacks are each at one *focus*. If the tacks are moved farther apart, the ellipse will become longer and narrower; if they are moved closer together, it will become more circular. Finally, when the two *foci* merge into one point, we have a circle again.

Kepler tried such an ellipse for the orbit of Mars, putting the sun at one focus and leaving the other one empty. . . .

---

[3]The Greeks, of course, had not thought in terms of a single all-powerful God. That idea had come from the Jews and had been taken over by one of their minor sects, the Christians. But by Kepler's time it had become so ingrained that he never even thought of questioning it.

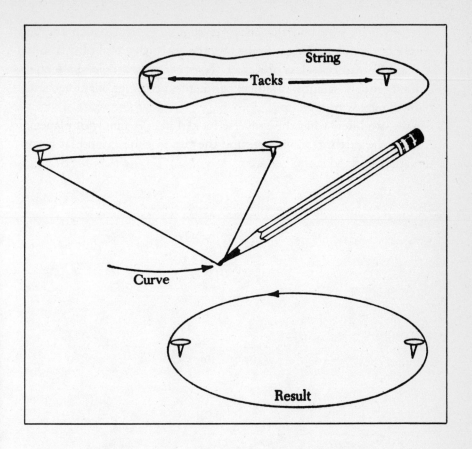

And he found a perfect fit with the observations of Mars. He did the same for all the other planets and found again a perfect fit. The planetary ellipses are very nearly perfect circles but not quite. Mars is the one planet in which the ellipse is noticeably different from a circle, and so it was the one planet whose observations didn't fit the calculations based on circular orbits.

But wasn't it weird? One could barely accept planets moving in circles, but moving in *ellipses?* Curiouser and curiouser the universe was becoming, as Alice would one day discover in Wonderland.

The Church was affronted, as were those who had followed the first scientific guidelines—beauty and simplicity. But the overwhelming logical appeal of testing ideas by experiment and observation carried the day against the beauty, simplicity, and sanctity of the circle.

And so finally we had the answer, thanks to the years of careful observations made by Tycho Brahe and the equally careful calculations and scientific stubbornness of Kepler. Together they provided a model for all subsequent science: careful experiments, precise calculations, and an unwillingness to give up.

Finally, we knew what the universe looked like. A family of planets, including the earth, revolving around the sun in ellipses, and far away the myriad of fixed stars.

FOUR
Law and Order

I. AS WITH ALL HUMAN ADVANCES, A PROBLEM OR two came with the new and correct model of the universe.

The first problem we have already discussed: It was the sudden opposition of the Church, which up until this time had been the somewhat flawed but the most important home of intellectual activity in Europe. The Church leaders found that they could not accept the new Copernicus-Kepler doctrine, with its planets moving in nongodly ellipses instead of perfect circles, and—even worse—with the earth as one of those meandering planets. For how could the Bible be interpreted other than that the earth is the center of all things? The whole biblical story of creation didn't make sense if it wasn't, and the thought of questioning the truth of the Bible was damned and damnable heresy.

This problem was at first the most terrible one. Galileo, Europe's greatest scientist in the early seventeenth century, brought out a further and invincible proof of the theory. Using the newly discovered telescope, he saw the moons of Jupiter revolving, not around the earth, but around that far-off planet. So clearly the earth could not be the center around which all motion revolved. Furthermore, he discovered that the planet Venus displayed different phases.

We are all familiar with the phases of the moon: Sometimes it is full and round, but periodically it thins to a crescent before growing full again. This is because, as it circles the earth, the sun shines on it from different angles as seen from earth: When the full face of the moon reflects sunlight to earth, it appears as full; and when only a thin arc around the edge reflects sunlight to us, it appears (to us) as a crescent. With his telescope Galileo found the same behavior for Venus. The difference between the moon and Venus, as seen from earth, is that

25

Galileo Galilei

Venus is always seen in close proximity to the sun, whereas the moon is often seen on the opposite side of the sky (around midnight). Galileo proved mathematically that we could see the different phases of Venus only if she were revolving around the sun rather than around the earth.[1]

[1]This is discussed in detail in *The Birth of the Earth.* (See bibliography at the end of this book.)

For his researches, Galileo was imprisoned by the Inquisition and threatened with torture and death if he did not recant his "damnable heresy," that the earth is not the center of the universe. Remembering the fate of Giordano Bruno and, indeed, that of thousands of hapless victims of the medieval heresy hunters who had been tortured and burned to death—for their own good, of course—he gave in and publicly stated that he no longer believed such heresy.

There is a legend that as he walked away after the public ceremony he muttered, "Nevertheless, the earth does move!" But the story remains, like those of the Golden Grail and the Sleeping Princess, nothing but a pretty legend.

2. The other problem raised by the Copernicus-Kepler model seemed at first much less formidable but turned out to be much more real. In the face of threats of torture and burning, most people ignored the new theory, but people eventually die. And as a new generation grew up in Europe, what had seemed terrible and heretical and impossible to their elders seemed to them no big deal at all. We see this over and over again in history, in fields as diverse as politics and art as well as science. Bernard Shaw was regarded as an evil rapscallion when he first began writing plays, but today it's hard to understand what all the fuss was about. When jazz came flowing out of New Orleans in the early years of this century, it was regarded by the older generation as an invitation to hell and depravity; today that role has been taken over by punk rock, and jazz is "respectable".[2] Democracy seemed to the ruling classes of England and France a most terrible heresy when the American colonies proclaimed it in the eighteenth century, but today those countries are among its stoutest defenders.

And so the Church threat simply faded away into the gloom and didn't bother people anymore. But there was this other problem.

In the Greek universe all observed motions were understandable on the basis of the principle of "natural motion": In the heavens everything moved in a perfect circle, while on earth everything fell down toward the center of the universe. And it all seemed to make sense. But now the earth was one of those wild planets cavorting around the sun. What possible significance could the center of such a moving body have? Why

[2]Punk rock, of course, really is depraved and wicked.

on earth should things fall toward that center? And the heavenly bodies themselves did not move in circles but ellipses. What could possibly make them do so? People could accept "perfect" motion in the heavens, but not imperfect: If the heavenly bodies weren't moving in circles, why should they move at all? And if they did move, why not in squares or triangles or simply back and forth at random? Why should God—or the gods or whoever—pick on the ellipse?

This question was nothing less than a demand for a whole new basic principle of the universe. The question was really: "What governs the universe?"

3. The answer was provided by Isaac Newton, who was born in England one year after Galileo's death in 1641. By the time Newton had graduated from college, in 1665, the Galileo-Church controversy had been largely forgotten, particularly in England, which didn't pay much attention to the Catholic Church anyway. More important in England was the bubonic plague, which returned in the year of Newton's graduation; it had been coming and going for the past several centuries, decimating whole populations and then disappearing without apparent reason. To avoid it, Newton returned to his hometown of Woolsthorpe instead of heading to London, where Cambridge graduates usually congregated.

In the next two years, in enforced isolation, he worked out in his own mind the laws that lay behind the order observed in the universe. He borrowed, as all good scientists must, the ideas of those who preceded him; he later said that if he had been able to see farther than most men, it was because he stood on the shoulders of giants. (He didn't, however, care to name those giants. He preferred that those who had helped him with their ideas remain anonymous while he reaped the credit.)

The basis of all his work is that there exists in this universe a set of laws that apply to *all* bodies, whether heavenly or earthly. The story that his concept of gravity was inspired by an apple falling on his head is probably just another one of those lovely legends, but there is meaning behind it. Because what he understood was that the same force that pulls the apple down from the tree to the ground, the same force that guides artillery shells and arrows and falling leaves, also guides the planets around the sun.

The ultimate democracy: one law for all.

28

FIVE
Gravity

I. THE PRINCIPLES ON WHICH THE UNIVERSE WAS based were about to be changed. For the concept of "natural" motions, which stated that heavenly bodies naturally moved one way while earthly bodies moved another, Newton now substituted the concept of natural laws that are everywhere the same and that must be obeyed everywhere in the universe.

One such law is *inertia,* which says simply that a body at rest will remain at rest unless a force acts on it, and that a body in motion will remain in motion in a straight line, again unless a force is applied.

Why? Why should objects prefer to be either at rest or in straight-line motion? What is so holy about a straight line or about rest? Why shouldn't objects move in curved lines or oscillate back and forth?

Newton gives no answer. A *physical law* is based on two things, ignorance and observation. By ignorance I mean that the law reaches up to the limit of our understanding, and if we try to look farther we see nothing; we are ignorant of any deeper understanding. If we understood the reason for the law, then that reason itself would replace the law.

By observation I mean that since we don't comprehend the reason for the law, we can't deduce it logically from first principles. Instead the law arises from observing how things behave in this universe. Newton simply pointed out to us that in this universe things at rest remain at rest, and things in motion keep moving in a straight line.

Of course, if the explanation really had been as simple as that, Newton would not have been the genius he was; *anybody* could have invented the law of inertia. But when we look at this world we live in, that sort of linear motion behavior is *not* what we see at all, is it?

We throw a ball into the air: It is certainly in motion, but it does not continue in a straight line. It rises as we throw it, and then it curves over

Sir Isaac Newton

and falls down. And how about an object at rest? If we hold a glass of water over our head, it is certainly at rest. Now if we carefully let it go—carefully, so as not to disturb it—does it remain there at rest, suspended over our head? Not quite.

So is Newton wrong?

No, because he also formulated other laws. The one pertinent in this case and also the one most important to our discussion is his law of *gravity*.[1] It states that between any two objects in the universe there exists an attractive force, proportional to the masses of each and inversely proportional to their distance.[2] This law can be written mathematically as

$$F = MmG/d^2$$

where G is a universal constant known as the gravitational constant, and the masses of the two objects, *m* and *M*, and their distance from each other, *d*, can have any value depending on the masses and distances involved.

So when we hold the glass of water over our head, a force is acting on it, attracting it to every other object in the universe. But since the force is larger depending on the mass of the other object and on where that object is, it should be obvious that in this case the biggest, closest object to the glass of water is not the person holding it or the furniture in the room or the car parked outside, but the entire earth itself. So the overwhelming force the glass of water feels is toward the earth. And so when we release it, it doesn't stay at rest *because there is a force acting on it*, and that force pulls it down to earth.

That's the same force that pulled the apple down onto Newton's head and the same force that keeps the moon circling the earth and the earth and other planets circling the sun. Newton's great achievement was to show that the heavens and the earth are not really separate but are integral parts of this one universe, governed by laws that operate equally everywhere in the universe.

But if this same law operates equally—this law that pulled the glass of water down onto our head and the apple onto Newton's—why doesn't it also pull the moon down onto our heads? Why doesn't it pull *us* down into the sun?

[1]This concept was actually first arrived at by one of Newton's rivals, Robert Hooke. Newton never gave him credit for his idea and generally receives credit for it because he was the one who put it into firm mathematical form and showed its importance in the universe.
[2]We won't go into the concept of mass. For our purposes we can regard it simply as the weight of an object.

2. Let's start by considering circular motion, with another *gedankenexperiment.* Suppose you have a bucket of water, with a string attached to the handle. You hold the bucket up over your head and slowly turn it upside down. You get wet. (See the advantage of the *gedankenexperiment* over actually doing it?) Now fill the bucket again and this time hold it by the string. And now quickly swing the bucket up and whirl it over your head, up and down, around and around. At the beginning a bit of water will spill out; but once you get the bucket whirling fast enough, the water will *not* spill out, even when the bucket is directly upside down over your head.

Why not? Because there is another force associated with circular motion, a force that comes directly from Newton's first law. Think of the bucket as it whirls. It is obviously in motion, and therefore it will remain in motion in a straight line. But it doesn't. Instead it curls around in a circle over your head. Why? Because you are exerting a force on it by pulling on the string. (You can *feel* this force as you whirl it.) This force is directed inward, from the bucket toward your hand. If you think of the bucket as traveling in a circle, then clearly your hand is the center of the circle. Such a force, present in all cases of circular motion, directed inwardly from the object to the center of the circle, is called *centripetal* force. It must be present, because if it is not, the object will travel, not in a circle, but in a straight line.

But if this were the *only* force, the object would move with it toward your hand instead of moving in the circle *around* your hand. This indicates that there is another force, exactly balancing the centripetal force and directed outward; we call it *centrifugal* force; it results from the bucket's desire to keep traveling outward in a straight line.

These forces are present in all circular motion. For example, they are responsible for the way you throw a baseball. You begin by whirling it over your shoulder. By holding onto it for a moment, you are exerting centripetal force; when you let go, the centripetal force disappears and the centrifugal force pushes it outward. With the disappearance of the centripetal force it no longer moves in circular motion, and Newton's first law takes over: It flies away from you in a straight line. (The straight-line motion doesn't continue forever, because the force of gravity soon takes over, bending its path down toward the ground.)

Now let's look again at the planets in their motion around the sun. They are in circular motion,[3] so there must be a centrifugal force pushing them away from the sun. Since they don't fly away, there must also be a centripetal force holding them in. But unlike the case of the water bucket whirling over your head, no string is attached to them. So what provides the centripetal force?

Right. Gravity. Just as you pulled, through the string, on the water bucket, the sun pulls—through gravity—on the planets. Using a form of mathematics he had invented himself, which today we call *calculus*, Newton showed that the centrifugal forces of the planets exactly balance their centripetal forces, and so they remain forever revolving around the sun. A precise calculation, in fact, shows that when the attractive force is inversely proportional to the square of the distance—as gravity is— then the motion of the revolving objects must be elliptical.

And so we have it: a complete description of what we now call the *solar system*—the sun and its planets—as it was known in Newton's time. In fact, we have a bit more than that; we have a clue to its origin. We have, indeed, for the first time in human history, the *necessity* to think about its origin. Because if the planets had been carefully placed in their orbits, the force of gravity would necessarily have pulled them straight into the sun! Somehow, when the solar system formed, the planets must already have been in circular motion. This is a thought we'll have to come back to when we discuss the origin of the earth, but first let's see how further, more careful observations led to a whole new concept of gravity—and indeed of our entire universe.

[3]All right, elliptical. But an ellipse is nearly a circle and also has the same forces associated with it. We'll come back to this point in a minute.

SIX

Relativity:
The Special Theory

I. FOR NEARLY THREE HUNDRED YEARS NEWTON RE-
mained on a pedestal as the undisputed giant of human intellectual
achievement. In the early years of the twentieth century he was joined
by Albert Einstein.

During the intervening years a host of scientists had built a magnifi-
cent structure of physics on the solid foundation of Newton's laws. But
by the end of the nineteenth century a slight problem was rising.

At first the application of Newton's laws to the motions of the planets
was straightforward. But when the astronomers began to build better
telescopes and make more precise measurements of the planetary positions, it became necessary to refine the calculations to see if the laws
could explain everything. And now the calculations became quite complicated, because the force of gravity exists between *every* two objects:
The earth is attracted to the sun but also to all the other planets. Since
the sun is so much bigger than the planets (all the planets together are
less than one percent the mass of the sun), the gravitational force the
earth feels is overwhelmingly due to the sun. Overwhelmingly but not
totally. In order to calculate the exact orbit the gravitational attraction
of the other planets must be considered. In particular, Jupiter is the
largest of the planets, and its attraction is the greatest.

In a similar manner, Jupiter's orbit is influenced by its massive neighbor, Saturn, and it in turn by Jupiter and Uranus. For all these planets,
when the disturbances caused by their neighbors were taken into account, the calculations based on Newton's laws exactly matched the
observed positions. And then, some two hundred years after Newton
had introduced his concept of gravity, a discrepancy was noticed in the
motion of Uranus. By this time everyone was so convinced of the truth

34

of Newton's ideas that they attributed the deviation of Uranus to the presence of an unknown planet, so far away that it had never been seen. With the aid of Newton's equations, they were even able to calculate exactly how big that planet must be and where it must be in order to affect Uranus in the way that it does.

And on September 23, 1846, a group of astronomers in Berlin looked for and found the planet, which they named Neptune. This was an exciting vindication, if any had been needed, of Newton's laws. And nearly a hundred years later, in 1930, the American astronomer Percival Lowell was inspired by deviations that had been noted in Neptune's orbit to look for still another planet, Pluto.

It turned out that the discovery of both planets had been more accidental than people had realized at the time. The available observations of both Uranus and Neptune were not sufficient to establish the new planets' exact positions in the sky, and so both discoveries depended a good deal on luck. By the time Pluto was discovered, however, its presence had already been overshadowed by another mystery: the precession of the perihelion of Mercury and the doomed planet Vulcan.

2. Vulcan wasn't exactly doomed; it simply never existed. It arose in men's minds because of the motion of Mercury.

Mercury is the innermost planet of the solar system. It is so close to the sun that, as seen from earth, it is nearly hidden in the sun's glare. It was therefore hard to make accurate observations of its orbit. By the end of the nineteenth century, however, the observations had become sufficiently accurate to show clearly that something was wrong.

The planets move in ellipses. But Mercury, when it finished its ellipse, didn't come back quite to the same point, as Newton had said it must.[1] The shift in orbit was quite small, but it was definite, and Newton's simple law couldn't explain it. The astronomers therefore believed that another planet must be even closer to the sun than Mercury. Its attraction was pulling Mercury out of its proper orbit, and it hadn't yet been seen because it was hidden in the glare of the sun.

But they could calculate that it must exist. They were so sure that they

[1]This is described by considering the point of closest approach to the sun of its elliptical orbit, the "perihelion." The perihelion moves, or "precesses," with each revolution.

even named it: Vulcan, after the Roman god of fire and heat.

And then they looked for it and looked for it.

But Vulcan just isn't there.

3. Einstein was not concerned with the Mercury-Vulcan problem. In the early years of the twentieth century he was finishing his schooling and growing from a boy into a man, and he was wondering about light. It's interesting to realize, since his name is always associated with the theory of relativity, that people had known for many centuries that motion is relative, and that Einstein's great contribution arose when he realized that in all the universe there is one motion that is *not* relative but is fixed, is *absolute.*

To understand what is sometimes called *Galilean relativity,* think of two people throwing a ball back and forth inside a jet airliner flying from Miami to New York. As they throw the ball, it moves with a speed of a few feet per second, which is about five miles per hour. But is that the "true" speed of the ball? It is also moving from Miami to New York at a speed of 600 miles per hour. Yet if the ball is going so fast, how could they catch it? After all, the fastest fastballs thrown by the greatest pitchers in the major leagues go just slightly more than *one* hundred miles an hour.

The answer is that relative to the people in the jet, the ball is going 5 miles per hour, while relative to the ground it is going 605 miles per hour when they throw it forward and 595 miles per hour when they throw it backward. This is simple Galilean relativity, otherwise known as addition (or subtraction) of velocities.

And what is the "real" speed of the ball? There is none. After all, it is going about 5 miles per hour relative to the passengers and 600 miles per hour relative to the earth, but the earth is whirling around the sun, so *relative to the sun* its speed is very different from either 5 or 600 miles per hour. And the sun is whirling through the galaxy, and the galaxy is whirling through the universe. . . . So what speed is the "real" speed? The best answer is simply to say that all motion is relative and to define the motion of the ball, you have to say who's measuring it. (When you hear a radio broadcast of a baseball game in which Wade Boggs slams a line drive over short, you don't want the announcer to start to describe the trajectory of the ball in terms of the sun's motion in the galaxy; you

Albert Einstein

want to know where it's going relative to the shortstop—over his head or into his mitt, right?)

But now consider the nature of light. There was a controversy at the time over whether light consists of particles (called photons) or waves. Newton had favored photons, but in the nineteenth century a physicist named James Clerk Maxwell had formulated a beautiful theory of light as a form of what we call *electromagnetic* waves, and the theory had explained the behavior of light so perfectly that it had convinced everyone of its truth. Einstein, however, was not convinced. (In 1905, the same year he published his theory of relativity, he also published a paper explaining an experiment known as the photoelectric effect, with the use of photons instead of waves. He was awarded the Nobel prize for this paper.)

If you think about it for a moment, you'll see that waves and particles are conceptual opposites. A particle can be thought of as a small baseball, while waves can be visualized as waves in the ocean. The basic point about a particle is that its surface defines where the particle is: It is everywhere inside that surface and nowhere outside it. A wave, on the other hand, has no such boundary. Drop a pebble into the ocean and watch the waves spread out. You cannot pick one precise point and say that the wave exists to one side of that point but not to the other; it simply gets smaller and smaller, until finally you can say it is no longer there—but you can't say precisely where it ceased to exist.

So which is light, a wave (as defined by Maxwell's theory and as "proven" by the many experiments that showed perfect agreement with that theory) or a particle (as defined by Newton and "proved" by Einstein's photoelectric effect)?[1]

The problem is that you can't see either the photons or the waves because they move so fast. It was known by then that light has a speed of 186,000 miles *per second,* incomparably faster than anything else in our everyday experience. And so it zips by so fast that we can't see if it is made of particles or waves. But suppose, Einstein said, that we *could* move along with it at that velocity. Then we could see it clearly enough to discern what it's made of.

Einstein finally came to the conclusion that it was impossible, that motion is a necessary part of the nature of light, and that light not in motion relative to anyone trying to observe it wouldn't be light at all.

The velocity of light had actually been a puzzle for some years. It should behave as all other motions behave: relative, or additive. If someone on a 600-mile-per-hour jet turned on a flashlight, the speed of the beam of light relative to the ground should be $186,000 \times 60 \times 60 = 669,600,000$ miles per hour *plus* 600, or 669,600,600. But in fact just a few years previously the speed of light had been measured quite

---

[1]You may notice that in the following discussion I give no answer to this question. That's because we don't know the answer, and so we speak of light—and of particles—as exhibiting a "wave-particle duality," which is another way of saying that we have come up against the limits of our present knowledge.

accurately by two Americans, Albert A. Michelson and Edward W. Morley—in the first scientific experiment of worldwide importance ever made in America—and they hadn't been able to find any difference at all in the velocity of light, whether it shone from a moving source or a still one.

Einstein now explained this result by saying that it needed no explanation; it simply was; the motion of light was the one motion in the universe that was *not* relative but was always the same, no matter who observed it or how the light was shone.

But by all the laws of physics then known, this wasn't possible. So Einstein said, "Let's change all the laws of physics."

4. It wasn't actually that simple or clear-cut. What he set out to do was to see if he could formulate a new set of physical laws that would allow the velocity of light to be always constant and still give agreement with all the experiments and observations that had been made up till then.

And he found that he could do it—if he gave up some basic assumptions that people had always accepted about the universe.

Time, for example, had to become relative: It must flow more slowly for people in motion than for those at rest. (The concept of *people* is not necessary; it is time itself that flows more slowly when whatever is measuring it is in motion.) This seems terribly weird but was proved in the 1960s, when two atomic clocks, which keep very precise time, were first synchronized perfectly—so that they showed the identical time—and then one of them was flown around the world on a jet. While it was in motion, according to Einstein, its time would slow down by a tiny fraction of a second so that when it came back to the other clock, it would be just that much slower. And it was.[2]

And he found other weird effects. Mass was no longer constant but relative. The mass of an object in motion was related to the mass of that same object at rest by the equation

$$m = m_o / \sqrt{1 - v^2/c^2}$$

where m_o is the mass of the object at rest and m is its mass when moving

[2]Other experiments had previously been done that proved this relativity of time even more exactly, but they need a more mathematical explanation.

with the velocity v, and c is the speed of light. According to this, if something is moving at 99 percent the speed of light ($v = 0.99c$), then

$$m = m_o/\sqrt{1 - (.99)^2 c^2/c^2}$$

$$= m_o/\sqrt{1 - (.99)^2}$$

$$= m_o/\sqrt{1 - .98}$$

$$= m_o/.14$$

$$\cong 7m_o$$

In other words, the object in motion is seven times more massive than the same object at rest. Which seems ridiculous, because a baseball when thrown doesn't become bigger or heavier. But don't forget, it's not going at 99 percent the speed of light. When the velocity is slow compared with the speed of light, the equation reduces to

$$m = m_o/\sqrt{1 - 0}$$

$$= m_o$$

which says that there is no change in the mass. So we can see such changes only when things go nearly as fast as light. We have seen the experimental proof of this in our giant atom smashers, where atomic nuclei are accelerated to such speeds, and indeed we can measure their mass increasing, just as Einstein said.

There are many other such weird results, and all of them have subsequently been confirmed by experiments. One you are probably familiar with is the fact that mass and energy turn out to be equivalent, through the most famous equation ever written:

$$E = mc^2$$

which tells us that mass can be converted into energy, which is what happens in our nuclear reactors to bring us electricity and which is what happened over Hiroshima and Nagasaki to bring an end to the Second

World War, saving millions of lives—although at the cost of nearly two hundred thousand killed in the nuclear explosions.

All these results came out of what Einstein called, in 1905, his *special theory* of relativity. He called it a special theory because, in order to simplify the mathematics, he had envisaged a universe with only a special kind of motion allowed: motion in straight lines at constant speeds. Without going through the mathematics, it should be clear that it was easier to deal with such simple situations than with the more complex—and more real—universe in which accelerated motions are possible. One of the necessary results was that the concept of gravity never appeared in his theory. This was because gravity imparts acceleration to bodies. (If you step out of a tenth-floor window, at the instant you leave the window you are barely moving, but you quickly begin to fall quite rapidly. By the time you splatter on the ground, you are moving very fast indeed. Gravity has accelerated you.)

Einstein realized, of course, that the omission of gravity was a serious neglect of his theory. Now, made confident by the success of special relativity, he devoted a dozen years to working out the complicated mathematics of a more general theory, one that would include accelerated motion and might thus lead to a new description of gravity.

When he succeeded, he had the *general theory* of relativity, and our world has never since been the same.

SEVEN
Relativity:
The General Theory

I. THE MATHEMATICS OF GENERAL RELATIVITY IS IN-
credibly complex, too complex to be described in a book like this. But
the concept of gravity that comes out of that mathematics can be as
simply described as it is conceptually weird.

Basically, the general theory is a *geometric* theory; it describes the
geometry of space and time. That doesn't sound terribly weird, except
that space—and time—turn out to be sometimes curved.

To explain that, let's first turn to the concept of dimensionality and
space. There are different kinds of spaces, which differ in their dimensions. The dimensionality of a space is the smallest number of directions
that must be given in order to locate a point within it, starting at any
point you like. For example, consider the space that consists of a line:

The X marks a point on that line. If I want to tell you where it is, I
could say that it is two inches from the origin of the line (marked with
an O). That one number defines the location of the point, so a line is
a *one-dimensional space.*

Now consider the surface of a dollar bill. If I want to tell you where
any point on it is (for example, the location of the tip of George
Washington's nose), I would have to give you *two* numbers: I could tell
you to start at the upper left-hand corner and then go down 3.15
centimeters and turn right 8.25 centimeters, and there you are. (I could
give you *different* numbers, for example, starting from a different corner
or combining one measure of length and one of angle, but I need *at least*
two numbers in each case to define any spot on the page.) The surface

of the dollar bill, like that of this page, is therefore a *two-dimensional space.*

The space we live in is three-dimensional: We need three numbers to locate an object in it. If an airplane is flying over the Atlantic Ocean, in order to locate it we need to know its longitude, its latitude, and also its altitude. Einstein pointed out, however, that if you go looking for that airplane the next day it won't be where those three numbers say it is. We actually need four numbers to describe its position accurately, the three space numbers plus the time. Time thus becomes our *fourth* dimension.

Even more important, Einstein's results from general relativity told us that normal space-time is not always flat but may be curved.

Let's go back now to Euclid. His summary of the old Greek geometry is still taught today in our schools, because it is still valid. A straight line, for example, is the shortest distance between any two points, right? The sum of the angles of a triangle must equal 180 degrees. But we learned in chapter 1 that if a triangle is laid out on a curved surface, that last statement is no longer true. And neither is the first one.

We live, in a sense, on a curved two-dimensional surface: the surface of a sphere, the earth. If we want to travel from New York to London by the shortest route, do we travel in a straight line? We do not; if we did, we'd end up out in space!

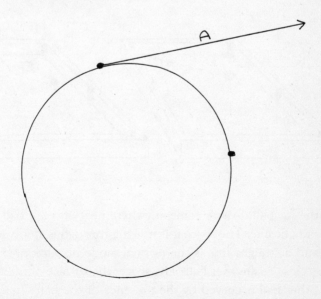

The straight line A would take us right off the surface of the earth, so instead we follow the curved surface. When something is *traveling in a curved space, the direction of motion must be curved.*

This is equally true of a curved three-dimensional space. (We'll forget, for the moment, the time dimension, in order to simplify our ideas.) The problem is, it is impossible for us to visualize a curved three-dimensional space. Einstein couldn't visualize it either; it's a basic limitation of our human imaginations. But it is gloriously true that our mathematical imaginations can fly way past our poor human capabilities, and so he was able to work out the consequences of a curved three-dimensional space.

He said, first of all, that empty space is flat. This means that the normal Euclidean propositions are true: The shortest distance is a straight line, the sum of the angles, and so on. But when *mass* is present, the space around that mass is warped, or curved.

To understand this, let's think of a two-dimensional analogy, since our minds simply can't handle curvature in three dimensions. So think of a billiard table. In fact, think of a *cheap* billiard table, where the surface can't quite hold the weight of the billiard balls, so that they sink into it just a bit.

On a normal billiard table, when the ball is hit with the cue stick, it moves in a straight line. What about this cheap table?

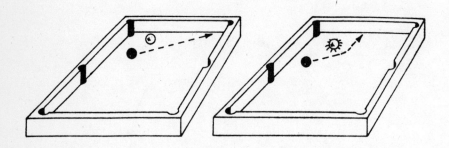

If the hit ball doesn't come anywhere near another ball, it will move in a straight line: The space it is moving through is empty and therefore flat, and a straight line is the normal mode of motion. But suppose it comes close to another ball. The space, the surface of the table, around that other ball is curved by the presence of the ball's mass. Therefore, as the ball enters this curved space (the indented table top), it will roll into it and *curve around the other ball.*

Now suppose that we can't see the indentures in the table and don't know they are there. What we would *observe* in this *two-dimensional universe* (the surface of the billiard table) is that when one ball approaches another, it curves toward it. But since we know—or think we do—that normal motion is in a straight line unless a force acts on the object (remember Newton's first law?), we would conclude that there must be a force acting on the ball that moves in a curve!

This is precisely the behavior we see in our own three-dimensional space. We throw a ball into the air. It does not move off in a straight line but curves back toward the earth. Newton told us that is because there is a force—gravity—acting on it. Einstein now tells us that the ball curves because the mass of the earth curves the space around it, and so the ball naturally moves in a curve. In the same way, the planets move in a curve around the sun—because the mass of the sun curves the space around it.

Gravity, in the general theory of relativity, appears naturally as the curvature of space.

2. Well, so what? We already had a perfectly good theory of gravity—Newton's—so what is the advantage of a more complicated theory? And Einstein's theory is indeed much more complicated; I couldn't even begin to write down the equations here, whereas Newton's equation for gravity was quite a simple thing (page 31). So according to Occam's Razor, isn't Newton's theory better?

But remember how we started all this discussion: There is a problem with Newton's theory—the motion of Mercury.

And when Einstein set down his complicated equations and solved them for the case of Mercury, he found that they agreed with the observations.

When Einstein's equations are simplified, they reduce to the same form as Newton's, so we conclude that Newton is correct but not so precise as Einstein. For most of the planets, Newton's equation is sufficiently accurate to describe their motion. But Mercury is the planet closest to the sun, and so the curvature of space is greatest there, and in that situation Newton is just not quite accurate enough.

But Einstein is.

3. That all sounds good enough, but let's remember the basic principle of science: testability. Before anyone was willing to accept such weird notions as the curvature of space, they demanded that this new theory be tested and proved.

Einstein agreed and told them how they could do it. According to Newton, gravity is a force between any two objects in the universe, depending on their masses: $F = GMm/d^2$. If the mass of any one of the objects is zero, then the force disappears. Does any object have a mass of zero? One does: the photon, the particle of light. Newton therefore concluded that light is not affected by the gravity of the earth or the sun or anything else: It always moves in a straight line.

And this is what we normally see. If we shine a flashlight beam up into the air, it doesn't curve around and bend down like a thrown baseball; it continues on up until it's lost from sight.

But Einstein said no. He explained that gravity is really a curvature of space, and in a curved space *everything* must move in a curved line. Because light is moving so fast, however, its curvature is very small and hard to detect. But it could be detected, he predicted, by watching it as it curved past something terribly massive, like the sun.

Suppose you're looking at a star in a flat space (which means there are no massive things, like other stars, within the space the starlight is traveling in on its way from the star to you). The light from the star then comes in a straight line to you. (The star shines out in all directions, of course, but you see only the beam of light that is headed directly into your eyes.) Now suppose that the sun rises and moves up toward that star you're looking at. When the sun reaches a point just next to the line of sight (between you and the star), it will curve that space, and the straight line along which the starlight moves will be curved. The result will be that the star will *appear* to suddenly jump, to change its position.

The problem is that when the sun rises, it is so bright that you can no longer see the stars. The solution Einstein proposed was to carry out the experiment during an *eclipse* of the sun. This occurs when the moon moves between the earth and the sun and blots out the sun. The sun is still there, still curving the space around it, but the sky is now dark, and the stars can be seen.

Einstein's theory was published in 1916, when Europe was caught up in the midst of one of the most horrible wars it had ever seen. Einstein was living in Germany, but a Dutch astronomer named Willem de Sitter sent a copy of his paper to Arthur Eddington in England. Eddington organized two British expeditions to test the theory: They would travel in 1919 to the southern parts of Africa and Brazil, where an eclipse was expected.

And so they did. Despite rather poor weather, they managed to take a series of pictures of the stars as the dark sun moved across the skies. And when they analyzed the pictures, carefully measuring the positions of the stars as the sun approached their line of sight, they saw indeed that in each case the stars moved, jumped, just as Einstein had predicted.

The president of the Royal Society, announcing the results to the newspapers, told them that an intellectual revolution had taken place, and that Einstein's achievement was "the greatest in the history of human thought." Einstein became the most famous person in the world (a fame he later shared with Superman).

Buoyed up by his success, he next applied his general theory of relativity to the entire universe.

And discovered that the universe didn't exist.

EIGHT
The Singularity

I. IT'S UNFAIR OF ME TO MAKE A BIG DEAL ABOUT that, because it turned out to be just a simple mistake, but it illustrates the usefulness of the scientific method. When Einstein first applied his new theory to the universe as a whole, he found that the equations couldn't be solved. Since the solution to the equations constitutes his description of the universe, the conclusion was that the universe didn't exist. If he had been founding a new religious cult, this might have been greeted with wild enthusiasm as a brilliant, new insight into reality. But science is based on testability, and since we observe the existence of the universe, any theory that tells us it doesn't exist does not agree with our observations and must therefore be discarded.[1]

Or at least the theory must be looked at again. The general theory of relativity was so successful in explaining Mercury's peculiar motion and the bending of starlight that Einstein and other physicists went over his calculations again and again, and in 1920 a Russian, Alexander Friedmann, found a simple mathematical mistake. (Yes, even Einstein could goof.) Friedmann went on to show that Einstein's equations did have a solution—indeed a solution with two important aspects.

The first thing was that if we traced the equations' solution back in time, we came up against what is called a *singularity*. This is a complex mathematical term, but in essence it means something that cannot exist in this universe. For example, if you watch the path of a thrown ball, you will see it describe a nice, smooth, curved line. That's fine. But if instead of that the ball suddenly disappeared and then a moment later reappeared, that would not be fine. Such behavior is impossible in this

---

[1]Unless, of course, Edgar Allan Poe was right when he suggested: All that we see or seem/Is but a dream within a dream.

universe. The moment of the ball's disappearance—and also its subsequent reappearance—would be a singularity.

So the fact that there was a singularity in the past behavior of the universe was bothersome. It looked as if there was something wrong, but in fact—as we shall soon see—this became the second clue we had to the origin of the universe.

The first clue was the other thing about the Einstein-Friedmann solution, which was that the solution was a function of time. That means that the solution—and therefore the universe it describes—depends on the time, which means the universe must be changing with time. In fact, it turned out that the universe was getting either larger or smaller as time went on. The theory wasn't specific about which, but certainly one or the other was happening.

The singularity was a difficult thing to deal with, since it had occurred so long ago, but the expansion (or contraction) of the universe was supposedly happening right now and so could be tested. Is the universe really getting bigger (or smaller)? This was something no one had ever suspected, and so if it could be proved, it would be convincing proof of the correctness of the Einstein-Friedmann universe. On the other hand, if it was not growing (or shrinking), then the solution must necessarily be wrong.

But how could we tell?

2. Just as we can tell when an ambulance or a police car is approaching. The sound of the siren tells us it's out there somewhere, and the rise in pitch indicates that it's getting closer. After it passes, the pitch winds down as it recedes.

This is an example of the Doppler effect, which depends on the change in *wavelength* of a sound because of its motion.

When a guitar string is plucked, it begins to vibrate; this is what produces the sound. A long string will vibrate with a longer wavelength than will a short string, and this difference in wavelength governs the pitch of the resulting sound.

The situation is similar with light, or electromagnetic waves. A short wavelength gives a different color, instead of pitch, to the resulting light. Short wavelengths give us blue light; long wavelengths give us red.

Now imagine a moving source of sound (or light) waves, emitting sound (or light) of a given wavelength. As it moves away from you, it continually emits these waves, and a listener traveling with the source will hear these sound waves exactly as produced. But what do you hear if you're standing still as it moves?

During the time in which the source is creating one wave, it is moving away from you, so that the length of the wave (relative to you) is stretched out. The result is that you hear a sound of longer wavelength and therefore of lower pitch. In the case of light, you would see light of longer wavelength and therefore of a redder color.

The stars emit light of particular wavelengths, and the Austrian physicist C. Johann Doppler suggested that we could tell if the stars were moving toward or away from us by carefully measuring the wavelengths. Any stars moving toward us would show shorter wavelengths; any moving away would show larger. In a universe in which all the stars are in random motion we would see both effects; in a universe in which the stars were fixed in space we would see no change in wavelengths at all.

The stars, as it turns out, are arranged in *galaxies*, each galaxy being a group of about a hundred billion stars. In our own galaxy, the Milky Way, we see small shifts toward both shorter and longer wavelengths as our own star, the sun, moves through the galaxy, gaining on some stars and receding from others.

But when Vesto M. Slipher in 1926 managed to measure accurately the starlight coming to us from far-off galaxies, he found that *all* the starlight was shifted to longer wavelengths, to redder colors. This is called the *redshift*, which means that all the galaxies in the universe are receding from us. In other words, the universe is expanding; it is getting bigger.

The prediction of this result by Einstein's theory of relativity has been called the most incredible scientific prediction of all time. Instead of living in a stationary universe, as the Greeks had envisaged and as everyone had always assumed, a universe that had existed since the beginning of time, we suddenly found that we were in an expanding universe.

And immediately people began to wonder what that meant in terms of an origin. For if the universe is getting bigger, then as we think back in time, it must have been smaller . . . and smaller. . . .

And for the first time, people had a scientific clue to the ultimate mystery: How did it all begin?

NINE
The Big Bang

I. BY THE END OF THE 1920s SLIPHER'S WORK HAD BEEN followed with an extensive survey of faraway galaxies by Milton Humason and Edwin Hubble,[1] who found not only that all galaxies are spreading apart, but also that the farthest ones are flying away the fastest.

This was the important clue. Because that is precisely the result you would get from a bomb. Imagine a photograph taken of a bomb exploding:

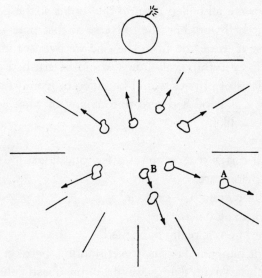

[1]During the long nights of star watching, these two used to amuse themselves by trying to compose complicated puns. They finally set the world's record with a triple pun: Three brothers started a cattle ranch, and when they asked their father to suggest a name, he replied, "Focus." Why? Because it's where the sons raise meat.

At the instant in time represented by the photograph, fragments will be flying all over. They will not all be the same distance from the center, from where the bomb originally was. This necessarily means that the pieces farthest away must be traveling fastest, because they all started out from the same place at the same time, at the moment of explosion.

When we look out at the galaxies and see them spreading apart and the farthest ones moving the fastest, we immediately begin to think perhaps we're looking at the remains of a gigantic cosmic explosion. George Gamow, a Russian-born American physicist, named it the Big Bang.

This theory says that the universe at some time in the past was all compressed into one huge ball, which then exploded. The universe we see today is still expanding outward with the force of that explosion.

The Big Bang is a direct consequence of Einstein's theory, which told us that the universe must be either expanding or contracting, and the observations of light from faraway galaxies, which is all redshifted. There is one other point, too: Einstein's singularity. No one knew what to make of it at the time; it seemed to be a flaw in the theory. But if today's universe were all balled up into one point at the beginning of time, that cosmic ball would *be* the universe at that time—and a very different universe it would be from the one we live in today. Gravity would overwhelm everything, all atoms would be crushed out of existence, the very laws of physics would be different from what we know today. And that's as good a description as any of what a singularity might actually look like.

2. Well, if all this is true, it raises a few questions. It seems to me that the most obvious are:
1. Why did the cosmic ball explode?
2. When did it explode?
3. How do we know it really happened?
4. Where did it happen? That is, if we, standing here on earth, look out and see all the galaxies flying away from us, doesn't that mean we are standing still right at the center of the universe? Doesn't that mean that the Greeks and the Church were right after all?

3. Let's take that last question first. We'll have to remember that we live in a curved four-dimensional space-time, and that our imaginations can't handle curved spaces of dimensionality larger than two. So let's envisage a *gedankenexperiment* about a curved two-dimensional space, like the surface of a ball.

It's important to realize that we're talking about only the *surface*. The ball itself, counting its insides, is a three-dimensional object. But the surface is two-dimensional since we can locate any object on it with only two numbers, latitude and longitude. And it's obviously a curved space, right?

Now since we want the space to expand, let's talk about a balloon instead of simply a rigid ball. We inflate the balloon until it swells into a round ball. Let's mark the curved two-dimensional surface all over with a grid of dots, equally spaced, one inch apart. And let's mark one of the dots—any one, chosen at random—by drawing a circle around it. Then we mark all the other dots with labels like a, b, c, d.. . .And finally we measure the distance, with a flexible tape measure, from our circled dot to each of the other dots, and we write down the distances. Now let's blow again into the balloon so that it gets even bigger.

What's happened to all the dots? Obviously, as the balloon swelled and grew, they moved farther from each other. Now each one is about two inches from its neighbor. Let's find the one dot we circled and again measure the distances from it to each of the dots a, b, c, d. . . .What's the result? Each distance is larger than it was when the balloon was smaller, isn't it? If you're not quite sure, try the real experiment. How much can a balloon cost?

The result is just what we see from earth when we look at the galaxies: On the curved surface of the balloon, each dot was receding from the marked dot as the balloon expanded, and in our curved universe each galaxy is receding from our earth. But was the marked dot on the balloon the *center* of the balloon? Of course not. Remember, we picked it at random. We could have picked *any* dot and found the same result: All the other dots would recede as the balloon expanded. And so the same must be true in our universe. As it expands, we would see the galaxies receding from us *no matter where we were standing*.

We can go even farther. Where is the center of the surface of the balloon? (Not the center of the balloon itself, which is a normal object in uncurved, three-dimensional space, but of the surface, which is a curved space.) Which of the dots could reasonably be called the center of the surface? None of them, of course. There *is* no center!

This is a characteristic of curved space: It has no center. If that seems hard to visualize, just think of the surface of the balloon. Or draw a circle. The circle itself is a flat object on a flat page, both the circle and the page being two-dimensional. But look at the *circumference* of the circle, the line that encloses it. Since it's a line, it has only one dimension and it is obviously curved. It represents a one-dimensional curved space. Where is its center? It can't be the center of the circle, because that point doesn't even lie on the line. Can you pick a point *on the line* that is its center?

You can't; no one can.

Because a curved space *has* no center. And neither has the universe.

4. Let's take the other questions in order.

1. Why did the cosmic ball explode?

This question represents a point beyond the limits of our present knowledge. The closest we can get to that moment of the Big Bang is to within a very short time *after* it happened; we don't yet know anything at all about what happened before that or why it happened. We have some speculations, though, which are tied in to the question of what will happen when this universe comes to an end—which it will some day—so let's put that question off until we discuss the Big End.

2. When was the Big Bang?

We have a fairly good answer to that—somewhere about fifteen to thirty billion years ago. It's an answer easy to find in principle but difficult in detail.

If we know how fast an object is traveling and how much distance it has traveled, then it's easy to calculate how long it's been traveling. If you are told that a car has been driving at 50 miles per hour steadily and has covered 200 miles, it shouldn't take you long to figure out that it started four hours earlier. Similarly, we measure the redshift of the galaxies, and that tells us how fast they are moving. If we can also measure their distances from us, we can easily calculate how long it has been since they—and we—were all together in one point.

The problem is that it is hard to measure the distances accurately, and so the best answer we have at the present is somewhere about twenty billion years ago, certainly more than ten billion and less than forty. As we build better telescopes, we'll be able to make more precise determinations of this age of the universe.

3. How do we know it's all true?

This question deserves a chapter of its own.

TEN

The Fireball Radiation

1. CONSIDER WHAT HAPPENS WHEN YOU TURN ON AN electric stove. The coils get hot and begin to glow red. When you turn it off, neither the color nor the heat disappears immediately. Someone coming into the room a few minutes later can tell the stove had been on by feeling its warmth or noting the still-glowing coils. We see the same thing in Western movies, when the scout discovers a still-warm campfire and knows he's on the right trail and not too far behind those he's after.

In much the same line of reasoning, in 1965 Robert Dicke of Princeton University was looking for the dying remnant of the Big Bang. He had calculated that the temperature at the moment of the creation of our universe must have risen to at least 10 billion degrees. Although 15 or 20 billion years had since elapsed, that was an incredibly high temperature, and he thought that some remnant would still be left—if one knew how to look for it.

But—how?

2. Arnold Penzias and Robert Wilson were physicists at the Bell Laboratories in New Jersey, not too far from Princeton. They were working on a distinctly different problem, trying to communicate with our new series of *Echo* satellites. The problem was that there was a disturbing background noise in the Bell system—a static—that they couldn't get rid of.

They knew their equipment was good; in fact, it was the most sensitive radio equipment that had ever been built at this wavelength (a few centimeters). So why did they have this damned static?

3. The fireball radiation, at the moment of the Big Bang, would have been of very short wavelength, corresponding to the incredibly high energies involved. But as the universe spread out and cooled down, the wavelength would lengthen. This would be due, not to the Doppler shift we discussed in the last chapter, but to the fact that the wavelength of emitted radiation is proportional to the energy (temperature) of the emitting body. If the coils on your electric stove could be turned up to higher temperatures, they would emit radiation of successively shorter wavelength, glowing orange instead of red, then yellow, and finally becoming white-hot. As they cooled, they would go through the colors again as their wavelength grew longer, dying out from white to red again before fading completely.

It was hard to tell what wavelength the original fireball would now have, for one thing because the exact time it happened was so uncertain. But Dicke was expecting a wavelength somewhere in the region of twenty centimeters or less. At wavelengths longer than about 20 centimeters, radiation from our present galaxy is so intense it would swamp the small fireball remnant, and at wavelengths less than 1 centimeter, the radiation is absorbed by the earth's atmosphere. So Dicke expected to find the answer somewhere between one and 20 centimeters.

4. What finally happened was that Penzias was discussing his problems with the strange static, talking it over with Bernard Burke of the Massachusetts Institute of Technology. Burke knew about Dicke's work and thought it possible that the Penzias problem might be the Dicke solution.

Penzias called Dicke and invited his group out to look at the Bell static, and when they observed it they were sure that they had found the last remaining vestige of the primordial beginning of our universe.

Static is generated in electronic equipment by many things, but most of these had been eliminated by the Bell group in their effort to attain the most sensitive possible communication with our satellites. One source of static that always remains is that generated by heat, because heat causes electrons to vibrate, and a vibrating electron emits electromagnetic radiation—static. If Dicke was right, then an inescapable source of heat pervades the universe: the heat left over from the Big

The Bell radiotelescope, which first measured the fireball radiation from the origin of the universe.

Bang. It is just the smallest bit of heat, corresponding to a temperature of only a few degrees absolute,[1] but it can't escape this universe. Dicke suggested that this is what was causing the Bell static.

The Bell machine, see photograph, measured the radiation at about 10 centimeters, at 7.3 centimeters, to be precise, while the Princeton group had been building an apparatus to look for it at 3.2 centimeters.

[1] The absolute, or Kelvin, temperature scale registers zero where there is no heat at all, which is −273 on the centigrade scale.

Knowing the Bell results, they were able to predict exactly how intense the radiation should be at 3.2 centimeters if indeed it was due to the leftover fireball radiation. Six months later they were able to make their measurements, and the Bell data were perfectly confirmed. Other labs followed suit at other wavelengths, and all their data fit the expectations exactly.

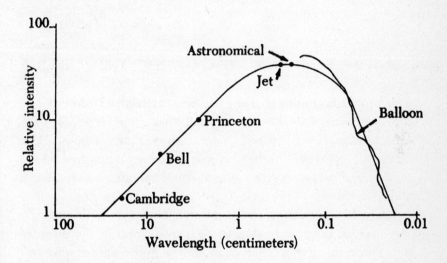

And so some twenty billion years after the cosmic fireball exploded, its faint remaining heat was detected on earth.

This radiation does not come to us from any discrete source; rather it is radiation that comes from space itself, that pervades the entire universe, that we see no matter where we look. It doesn't come from the stars, but from the empty space between the stars. Called by many names at first, but now known usually as the fireball or cosmic background microwave radiation, it is direct evidence of the origin of the entire universe.

There is no other possible explanation for the precise fit of the wavelength and the intensity of the measured radiation. And so today, whirling through the universe on our own little planet, after thousands of years of speculation and argument and wondering, of religion and poetry and mythology, we now know how the universe began.

ELEVEN
Fields and Forces

I. BUT WE STILL DON'T KNOW WHAT THE UNIVERSE really *is*.

We said at the beginning that the universe can be described in terms of things or principles. We know pretty well what our universe looks like in terms of things. It is composed of stars, grouped into galaxies, about a hundred billion galaxies in the universe, and about a hundred billion stars in a typical galaxy. At least one of the stars, our own sun, has a family of planets.

We don't know everything in these terms, of course; for example, it is likely—though unproved—that there is more mass in the universe in a state currently invisible to us than there is in the stars that we see. Such mass might be in the form of dark clouds of dust that we can't see in the blackness of space or in tiny, invisible particles called neutrinos or in black holes (to be discussed in part 2). Even more important, we don't yet know much about the universe in terms of basic principles.

When Newton taught us about gravity, about invisible universal forces, it seemed to many people he was preaching a doctrine that was taking us along on a dangerously backward journey. For what was gravity but an invisible force acting through no known mechanism? How could a sun 98 million miles away from us affect us without actually touching us in any way? It seemed as nonsensical as the theories of the astrologers.

We know now that Newton was right—or nearly right—but we still don't know how gravity operates. Einstein tells us that it is a curvature in space, but do we really understand that? Our minds can't really comprehend either Newton's action-at-a-distance or Einstein's curvature of space-time. But mathematically both descriptions can be formalized in terms of a concept called a *field*.

This concept was introduced by Michael Faraday in the nineteenth century to explain the force of magnetism. Imagine that you are holding two strong magnets, one in each hand. As you bring your hands closer together, you will begin to feel the magnets attracting each other; if they are strong enough, they will actually pull your hands together no matter how hard you try to keep them apart.

Think about this. When the magnets are far apart, say, on opposite sides of the room, there is no observable interaction between them; and yet when they come closer and are only a few inches apart, you can *feel* them pulling each other. But how does the one magnet know when the other magnet has come close? They're not touching, so how can they "communicate" with each other?

Now imagine you are holding two sticks, each tied to one end of a rubber band. If the band is loose, you can put the two sticks down on the table and nothing will happen; but if you do this when the band is stretched tight, the two sticks will fly toward each other. If you hold them with the band stretched tight, you can *feel* them trying to rush together, just as the magnets do. Again in this case the two sticks are not touching, but it is clear how they each "know" the other stick is there: by the action of the stretched rubber band attached to both of them. Through the band they "touch" each other.

In the same manner Faraday suggested that both magnets are touching by means of an invisible field. It is exactly as if they are connected by an invisible, stretched rubber band we call the *magnetic field*. Similarly, there exist electric fields and gravitational fields. It is the effect of the sun's gravitational field, through which the earth moves, that constrains its path around the sun. Whether you wish to call this effect a force or a curvature of space doesn't really matter; they are only different words for the effect of the field. (Of course, the proper mathematics *does* matter, and we have seen that Einstein's mathematics is the proper one to describe the gravitational field.)

James Clerk Maxwell followed up Faraday's concept by showing that the magnetic and electric fields were really only variations on a single kind of field; his work united them into what we now call the *electromagnetic* field. We know today four basic kinds of field in the universe, corresponding to the four types of force that govern all actions: gravity, electromagnetism, and the strong and weak nuclear forces.[1] At the present time we strongly suspect there is only one kind of field, which we describe in these four manifestations only because we don't yet understand it perfectly enough to describe it as one thing. In the past decade we have made much progress in uniting the four, but we are still far from there. An electroweak theory unites electromagnetism with the weak force, and the theory of the strong force is similar enough to give hope that it will soon be incorporated. But gravity seems to lead us into a totally new ballgame, unless a new class of theories known collectively as superstring and described in the next chapter, turns out to work.

2. This is what the universe is in terms of principles. It is even argued that everything in the universe is only a manifestation of these fields; the very atoms of which we are composed are thought of by some as being simply anomalies in the distribution of these fields.

Now that doesn't make any more sense to me than it does to you. Obviously we are talking about things we don't yet understand. In the next section we will talk about our universe in terms that we *do* understand, in terms of atoms and stars, and how these were created and have evolved into their present state. But before we do, let's spend a bit of time beyond the present edge of knowledge; let's talk about things we don't quite understand.

Such questions turn out to be such fun that they have led some scientists to an even wilder speculation: What is so holy about three dimensions for space? Could not other dimensions as well as other fields and forces exist?

This question arises because mathematicians find that they can solve equations in any number of dimensions, and the number three doesn't seem to be anything special. So why was the universe made with just three dimensions (plus one for time)? Couldn't other universes with more or fewer dimensions exist, with different kinds of fields instead of gravitational, electromagnetic, and nuclear?

For the answer to these questions, we must go back to the first syllables of recorded time. . . .

[1]To be discussed in part 2.

TWELVE
The First Moments

I. THE SINGULARITY AT THE BEGINNING OF TIME CAN be thought of as a state of infinitely high density, concentrated in a point of zero volume. A point of zero volume doesn't really take up any space at all, and if the singularity doesn't take up any space, then it doesn't really exist. That is lucky, because a state of infinite density doesn't correspond to any reality we can deal with. What we are really saying is that we don't understand what a singularity is or what the laws of nature are that govern it. At that initial point of time we pass into a different universe, one that is beyond our present state of knowledge.

We can, however, go back in time nearly up to that point, with varying degrees of understanding. Let's do that, starting with the first moment of the Big Bang.

2. The newest theories, called *inflationary*, are not in any sense proved by observation, but they're interesting and seem to make sense; that is, they are logical with no obvious contradictions. The first inflationary model was suggested by Alan Guth of M.I.T. in 1980; improved versions have been put forward by Andreas Albrecht and Paul Steinhardt of the University of Pennsylvania and by Andrei Linde of the Lebedev Institute in Moscow. The scheme has two basic ideas. One is that, in the first infinitesimal fraction of a second after the Bang, the universe expanded so wildly that different regions lost contact with each other. The other idea is that in the beginning only one force was in the universe, but it was soon broken up into the four basic ones we see today. How did that happen?

The ideas are incompletely worked out as yet but rest on there being properties of the early universe that break down the field of the basic

63

force into different forces. This breakdown cannot occur at very high temperatures, such as those that existed at the very beginning, when the universe was in its singularity state. But then the universe went through its inflationary stage, and as it expanded, it began to cool down from its initial infinite temperature, and the breakdown of the universal force into different forces took place.

Why did it break down into precisely the forces we see today—gravity, electromagnetism, and the weak and strong nuclear forces? Well, that's the interesting point about all this. There seems to be no reason for it, and it could easily have happened differently. In fact, the theory goes on to say that since different regions of the expanded universe lost touch with each other, as they cooled each of them might have brought into play different properties, which would then have resulted in different forces!

In effect, each of the regions of space, called *domains,* would be larger than the farthest distance we can see from earth, and since they might have different forces governing them, they would each have different laws of physics. They would be, in effect, different universes!

In this picture, the universe as a whole can be thought of as a dish of warm salt water, if you'll bear with me for a moment. Take a dish of warm water and pour salt into it; mix it up until the salt dissolves. Then let it sit. By the next day you should begin to see crystals of salt forming at the bottom, and if you let it sit in the sun for a few more days, all the water will evaporate and the dish will be full of salt crystals.

Our universe is one of those crystals. Everything we see—stars, planets, grass and people, viruses and rock musicians—are all within the one crystal that we call our universe. But in actuality—if this theory is right—the universe we call our own is only one of many crystals in the dish. Of course each crystal in our dish of warm water is similar and has formed by the same laws of physics, since all of them are in our own universe. But they are pointed in different directions, and though similar they are not identical. The different domains of the universe would be much more unlike, since the basic laws of physics would be different in each one.

How different? What would the effects be? If we were to travel from our own domain to another one that had different forces, what would happen to us?

We can't know; we have no possible way of knowing. Maybe, someday, we'll get a clue, but today I couldn't even begin to guess at the answers.[1] Instead, let's go on to the other question I mentioned earlier, the question of the dimensionality of reality.

We live in a universe of three space dimensions plus one of time. But mathematically nothing is particularly special about the numbers three or four, so why does our universe have just those particular numbers of dimensions?

The newest theories of particle physics, the science that attempts to determine the ultimate reality of the particles that comprise our atoms and, ultimately, our universe, are called *grand unified theories*, or GUTS, because they try to encompass in a single unified theory all the forces we see: gravity, electromagnetism, and the weak and strong nuclear forces.

Until very recently, all such attempts foundered on the rock of gravity: Attempts to incorporate it into any unified theory produced infinities in the solution, meaning that the solutions turned out to be absurd and without meaning. The beginnings of what seems as if it may be a proper solution came with the concept of *supersymmetry*.

Our description of nature has many symmetries, reflecting balances between such things as directions or forces or objects. We know that all objects are made up of atoms, and these in turn are composed of even smaller particles (as discussed on page 72). It may be difficult to visualize, but the revolution in our thinking that began with quantum theory tells us that forces, too, can be thought of in terms of particles. For example, the basic particle of the electromagnetic force is the photon, and that of gravity is the graviton. Supersymmetry is a postulated balance between the two basic groups of particles, *fermions* and *bosons*. Fermions include the basic particles of matter, electrons, and quarks (see chapter 13); bosons include the basic particles of forces, such as photons and gravitons. Supersymmetry postulates that a symmetry exists between the two groups, so that for every fermion there is a partner boson, and vice

---

[1]It may seem terribly unfair to raise interesting questions and then not answer them. But science is more important for the questions it raises than for the answers it provides. If you will let questions such as these simmer and fester in your mind, perhaps one day you may break out with a new direction for science to take, with the answers to these questions—and perhaps even with new questions.

versa. The bosonic partners to the electron and quark are called the selectron and the squark; the fermionic partners to the photon and graviton are called the photino and the gravitino.

These proposed partners have *not* been observed, but if one provisionally accepts them, things get interesting. The next step was taken when John Schwarz in America and Joel Scherk in France suggested that we should go right to the heart of all our theories, in which the basic particles of matter are thought of as points, or little infinitesimal balls. They suggested instead that the basic particles that form our atoms are not points at all but one-dimensional strings of zero thickness with lengths about 10^{-33} centimeters.[1] This makes them as small compared with our atoms as the atoms are compared with the entire solar system! When the concept of strings is joined with the supersymmetrical idea of pairing bosons and fermions, it turns out that the bosonic and fermionic terms cancel each other out so perfectly that no infinities remain in the resulting description of gravity; normal, finite, "real" results are obtained from the equations.

The theory, called *superstring* theory because of its connection with supersymmetry, suggests that all different forms of material reality are created by the vibrations, connections, and openings and closings of the strings. Actually several different superstring theories have been developed, with such names as SO(32) and $E_8 \times E_8$, depending on the specific characteristics of symmetry that they describe; those two, at least, seem to work—in the sense that they give solutions without infinities, which may well represent the real world. The former envisages strings that can be open or closed, while the latter works with only closed strings. There

---

[1]This system of notation is used quite a bit in science, so let's go over it. The number *one hundred* can be written as 100 or as 10^2, the number *one thousand* as 1,000 or as 10^3, etc. The exponent of ten tells you the number of zeros used in the more normal way of writing numbers. This method, called *scientific notation*, is useful when you get to very large or very small numbers. One trillion, for example (1,000,000,000,000) is written and comprehended more easily as 10^{12}.

For very small numbers we use negative exponentials. The decimal *one-tenth* is written as 0.1 or as 10^{-1}; *one-thousandth* is 0.001 or 10^{-3}, etc.; the exponential number tells how many decimal places are needed. We can see the advantage right away when we talk about the size of superstrings. Isn't it harder to say that they are 0.000000000000000000000000000000001 centimeters long, than to say they are 10^{-33} centimeters?

may well be other superstring theories; it is to be hoped we'll eventually find just one that is *real*.

These theories have one particular characteristic that tends to shock people, and well it might, because in order for the theories to be mathematically consistent, they insist that the universe exists in *nine* spatial dimensions instead of our normal three. The theories suggest that in the inflation of the universe that took place in that first moment, the three dimensions we are familiar with expanded with the universe, while the other six were left behind, remaining so small that we don't observe them (whatever that means). The other dimensions still exist but are coiled up so tightly that they have for all practical purposes disappeared; "our" universe, the one we see and feel and experience, has only the remaining three (plus time).

But why? Why have we been left with just three? Why not four or five or any number from one to nine?

Again, the answer seems to be that different domains in the universe might have any of these numbers of dimensions, just as they might have different laws of physics; in fact, almost certainly a relation exists between the forces and the dimensionalities that emerge in different domains.

But . . .

Our "universe" is necessarily restricted to three dimensions, because if it were not, we would not exist.

3. That is, we could not exist as creatures of flesh and blood living on a stable planet warmed by the sun.

Consider first the force of gravity that keeps our planet circling the sun. Its strength depends on the inverse square of the distance ($F = GmM/d^2$). It can be shown that in a four-dimensional space, it would depend on the inverse cube of the distance; in an n-dimensional space, it would depend on the n-1 power of the distance. But only if it depends on the *square* of the distance is it possible to find solutions to the equation that give stable planetary orbits around a massive body like the sun. So while it is possible that other domains of the true universe have more or fewer dimensions, they cannot also have planetary systems—and without planetary systems no life form remotely similar to ourselves can exist.

Is it possible that there might exist life, or consciousness of some sort, without physical bodies? Perhaps some sort of pure energy or pure something else that we can't even guess at?

Perhaps. But such speculation goes so far beyond the boundaries of our present science that we can't even begin to apply the basic principle of our method: testability. I'm afraid I feel—though it is and may forever remain impossible to prove—that no life at all would be possible in such domains, and therefore though such domains may indeed exist, no one will ever know.

Sad, isn't it?

Or, perhaps, wonderful . . . ?[3]

---

[3]The aspect of superstring theory that is most objected to is, in fact, not the extra six dimensions, but the lack of testability. At the present time we see no way of carrying out experiments that would test the various models; the experiments that can be envisaged require expenditures of energy well beyond our present resources. To say the least, this is regrettable; to say the most, it is unacceptable.

PART II

THE REST OF TIME

THIRTEEN
Atoms and Elements

I. EVERYTHING WE SEE IN THE UNIVERSE TODAY IS made up of some combination of less than one hundred different elements, and each element is made up of individual *atoms.* The word *atom* is Greek, going back at least to the fifth century B.C., but though the concept has a long history, it did not find easy acceptance, and for good reasons. You might as easily believe in tiny, invisible, green men with long noses and crooked smiles sitting on your shoulder as believe in tiny, invisible atoms. There are so many wild possibilities of existence in this weird universe that the person seriously interested in knowing the truth should believe only things for which evidence exists.

The difference between little, invisible, green men, and atoms is that we do have proof for atoms, and they actually do exist. The first proof of their existence didn't come until this present century, when Einstein gave a theoretical proof based on the observable motion of small particles in colloidal solution. A few years later Lord Rutherford carried out an experiment that not only proved their existence but also showed us what they look like, although they are too small to be seen.

Ernest Rutherford was a New Zealander who began his scientific career at Montreal, Canada, and Birmingham, England, before taking over the Cavendish Laboratory at Cambridge and making it into one of the world's best. To find out what atoms looked like, he directed a stream of alpha particles—which are subatomic particles emitted in the radioactive decay of radium—at a thin foil of aluminum. By observing the directions in which the alpha particles bounced off, he concluded that atoms consist of small, positively charged nuclei surrounded by clouds of electrons.

Contrary to the Greek idea, the atoms are not indestructible, although they are nearly so. The normal reactions of our world—such as melting and dissolving, boiling and freezing, crushing and eating, living and dying and decaying—can not destroy the individual atoms. The atoms of which Julius Caesar was composed are still in existence on this earth, dispersed around the globe by this time, and in fact by now some of them are almost certainly within each of us.

Nor are the atoms the smallest particles of which the universe is composed. Starting at the smallest, which we understand rather well, we have electrons and quarks. The quarks do not exist individually, but in groups of three they form either positively charged protons or neutral neutrons, which together form the nuclei of atoms. Outside that nucleus rotate clouds of negatively charged electrons.

Elements are defined by the number of protons in their atoms, with the number of electrons always equaling the number of protons. The simplest atom is hydrogen, with one proton, zero or one neutron, and one electron. The two types of hydrogen (one neutron or none) are called *isotopes* of hydrogen. The next atom is helium, with two protons, two electrons, and again two isotopes, in this case having either one or two neutrons. In this way, adding one proton and electron at a time (so that the atom remains electrically neutral), more and more complicated atoms are formed. The ones most important to us are hydrogen; carbon, with 6 protons; oxygen, with 8; and a few others up to iron, with 26.

All of the atoms mentioned so far are *stable*; in accord with the ancient Greek ideas, they are (virtually) indestructible. But each one of them has further isotopes, with greater or lesser numbers of neutrons, which are *unstable,* or *radioactive*; they spontaneously break down into stable atoms by emitting electrons or a combination of protons and neutrons called an *alpha particle* plus energy. The heaviest atom that occurs naturally on earth is uranium, with 92 protons, but all its isotopes are radioactive. The heaviest stable element is bismuth, with 83.

2. Now then, where did all these atoms come from?

For the answer to this question we have to start with the Big Bang. We don't understand the laws that governed the primordial lump that exploded or that first instant of the explosion when the temperature was presumably infinite, but we have some good ideas for everything that's happened since.[1]

To give you an idea of how close we can get to that initial moment of ignorance, let's think about the first thing that happened: the inflation of the universe that we talked about in the last section. That tremendous inflation, which may have separated the universe into separate domains and which structured our own universe (or domain) into what we see today, took how long, do you think? Millions of years? Billions?

It actually happened in the first infinitesimal part of one second! The best estimates are that the universe inflated in just the first 10^{-30} of that first second, and from then on we are dealing only with our own domain of that universe, which for simplicity we will refer to as "the universe." The first point at which we really begin to understand anything was reached when the density of matter fell to that of the density within a nucleus today, about 10^{14} grams per cubic centimeter. (A teaspoon of water at that density would weigh more than one million *tons*.) This happened when the time had reached 10^{-4} (0.0001) seconds and the temperature of the universe was about 10^{12} degrees absolute.

For the next moment, up until $T = 0.01$ second, the universe was dominated by radiation instead of matter; it was composed of a billion times more photons than protons or neutrons at a temperature of about 10^{11} degrees (about one hundred billion degrees). In this hot, radiation-dominated universe, electrons were continually coming into and passing out of existence; radiation at such high energies has the capacity to transform itself spontaneously into two particles, an electron and its *antiparticle*, the positron (a positively charged electron). The two particles, when they appear, fly away from each other, but if either of them encounters its antiparticle, they annihilate each other back into radiation.

In addition, the universe was full of neutrinos. These are tiny, massless or nearly so, particles produced today in radioactive processes. When a neutron decays to a proton and an electron, as it will in a few minutes

---

[1] Well, not everything, of course. We don't understand how Hitler or Vietnam could have happened; we don't understand love and hate or why music is beautiful, but we do have some pretty good ideas about what's been happening in the physical universe.

if left alone, it also produces a neutrino.[2] Since in nature any reaction that occurs can be reversed, it turns out that if a neutrino hits a neutron it can change it into a proton and an electron, or if one hits a proton it can change it into a neutron and a positron. In this early moment of the universe all such reactions were taking place.

The electron-positron pairs were continually being produced because, since $E=mc^2$, energy and matter are equivalent and, at a temperature of 10^{11} degrees, the energy of the radiation was roughly equivalent to that of the electron-positron pair. Thus mass-energy could pass from the form of energy to the form of matter easily enough. The mass of the proton and neutron, however, is about two thousand times greater than that of the electron (or positron), and so the radiation did not have enough energy to create protons and neutrons.

By $T = 0.1$ seconds the temperature had fallen to 3×10^{10} (30 billion degrees), and about two-thirds of the heavy particles in the universe were protons, only about one-third being neutrons. This is because the neutron is slightly heavier than the proton, and as the temperature dropped, it became harder for a neutrino to change a proton into a neutron than a neutron into a proton.

By $T = 1.1$ seconds the temperature was down to 10 billion degrees, and there were three protons for every neutron in the universe. A few seconds later the energy had dropped so low that no more electron-positron pairs were being produced. A few minutes later the temperature reached 1 billion degrees, and less than 15 percent of the nucleons (neutrons and protons) were in the neutron form. At precisely 3.75 minutes after the Big Bang, if the calculations are right, the temperature had dropped to 900 million degrees, and protons and neutrons began to fuse together to form the nucleus of a new atom, that of helium.

Within another minute the temperature dropped so low that the fusion reaction stopped, and the universe from that point on was pretty much what we see today. About 25 to 30 percent of the protons had been converted into helium, and the remaining neutrons decayed radioactively into protons and electrons. As the universe continued to cool, the electrons were attracted into stable orbits around the protons and

[2]There is actually a whole family of neutrinos and antineutrinos, but the differences among them are minor for our purposes.

the helium nuclei, and we ended up with a universe composed of about 73 percent hydrogen and the rest helium.

All this took place within the first few minutes. The next stage, the creation of the other ninety elements and the planets and stars and us, took millions and billions of years.

FOURTEEN

Stellar Nucleosynthesis A:
Hydrogen to Helium

I. *NUCLEOSYNTHESIS* MEANS THE SYNTHESIS, OR formation, of atomic nuclei. In the Big Bang this happened step by step, at the very high energies then available. First a proton and a neutron banged into each other to form the heavy isotope of hydrogen called deuterium. (This is the only isotope with a separate name. Isotopes are generally named after the element, with a number to indicate the total number of neutrons plus protons in the nucleus. Thus normal hydrogen is hydrogen-1, and deuterium—sometimes also called heavy hydrogen— is hydrogen-2.)

The proton and neutron are held together by the *strong* nuclear force. This is not only the strongest force in nature but also the one with the shortest range. It is only when the proton and neutron get to within about 10^{-12} centimeters of each other that they feel the force; once they do, they are permanently stuck together.[1]

Another neutron can join them to form hydrogen-3, which is radioactive but will last for years before it decays, but that is the end of the neutron addition process for hydrogen. No heavier isotopes exist. Alternatively, a proton can join the deuterium to form the new element helium, the isotope being helium-3. Finally, a proton can join with hydrogen-3 to form helium-4, or a neutron can join with helium-3 to make helium-4. A necessary part of the process is the addition of a proton, either to hydrogen-3 or to hydrogen-2, but the increase is hindered by the action of another of the basic forces, electromagnetism.

The electromagnetic force can be either attractive or repulsive; the rule is that like charges repel, unlike charges attract. You can see this in the magnetic form if you take two bar magnets. One end of each

---

[1]Unless blasted apart by giant atom smashers or, in the heaviest atoms, by radioactivity.

magnet will alternatively attract or repel the other magnet, depending on which end it is placed in contact with. The same is true for electric charges, and since all protons have positive charges, they repel each other. So when a proton comes flying up against either hydrogen-2 or hydrogen-3, it is repelled by the proton already there. (The neutrons, having no charge, are not affected.)

Since the nuclear force is stronger than electromagnetism, it can hold the protons and neutrons together inside a helium nucleus, but since it has such a short range, it can't be felt until the protons are pushed inside, past the repelling effect of the electromagnetic force. This takes tremendous energy, which was available in the early universe during the first four minutes. After that the temperature had dropped to the point where the universe had run out of sufficient energy and no more nucleosynthesis took place.

The process stopped at helium-4 because no nucleus of mass 5 exists, for reasons too complex to go into here. For the next several millions of years the universe consisted primarily of hydrogen and helium nuclei, around which electrons settled to form stable atoms. These primordial hydrogen and helium atoms continued to expand, with the force of the Big Bang pushing them along, and for a long time nothing much of interest happened.

Eventually, however, another basic force began to make itself felt.

2. Gravity.

It's an attractive force, remember, that exists between every two objects in the universe. As the cloud of hydrogen and helium expands and flies outward, it will be roiling with turbulent motion and eventually a number of hydrogen and helium atoms will come within reach of their respective gravitational forces.

Let's forget about the helium for a while, since at first it's the hydrogen that's important. Consider a mass of hydrogen atoms that happen to come close enough to each other for their mutual gravitation to hold them together. Each of the hydrogen atoms in this cloud is swirling away like mad in random motion, and between each pair of atoms is the attracting force of gravity. If the force of their random motion is great enough to overpower the gravity, then the atoms will simply fly away from each other and continue to meander through the expanding universe and need not concern us here. But if the force of gravity for this particular cloud happens to be enough to overcome the atoms' random motion, then they will be held together as a group—and then they become important.

If the gravity is even just slightly greater than that necessary to hold the atoms together, it will begin to pull them slightly closer together. And now an irreversible process begins. Because once they come closer together, the force of gravity becomes even stronger since it is inversely proportional to the square of the distance between each pair of atoms, which is now decreasing. Being stronger, it now pulls them together even harder, the distance decreases further, and as the process grows it snowballs into an avalanche of hydrogen atoms all falling toward each other—that is, toward the center of the cloud.

This increase of gravitational energy is turned into an increase in temperature as the cloud collapses; it gets hotter and hotter, eventually becoming so hot that the electrons are boiled off the atoms. The hydrogen nuclei—bare protons now—continue to fall together toward the center, accompanied but not interacting with the sea of electrons that surround them until they begin to collide with each other.

Here the electromagnetic force takes over, repelling the positively charged protons as they collide. But as the process of infall continues, the protons move faster and faster until finally they collide with equivalent temperatures of nearly one billion degrees, and the resultant energy—fed to them by the gravitational field—is sufficient to force them in past the repelling electromagnetic field.

They are, in fact, squeezed closely enough together that the strong nuclear field can take over—which it does, because it is the strongest of all—and the two protons are held tightly together by its force.

Now the final force comes into play. The *weak* nuclear force governs the distinction between proton and neutron. We have said previously that the neutron, left to itself, will decay radioactively to a proton plus an electron. In the same manner a proton, under certain circumstances, will decay into a neutron and a positron. The proton can't do it by itself, since it has less mass than does a neutron, but given the additional energy of being bound with another proton, it can. So one of the two protons decays into a neutron and a positron, the positron flies away (eventually meeting an electron and annihilating into photons), and the new nucleus settles down as hydrogen-2 (one proton and one neutron). The process continues with two more protons and ends, as in the Big

Bang, with the formation of an atom of helium-4.

The conversion of four protons into one helium-4 nucleus is important because the mass of the four protons is *greater* than the mass of the resulting helium-4. What happens to the missing mass? It is converted into energy, according to $E = mc^2$. This provides, at the very center of the collapsing cloud where most of the reactions are taking place, a new source of energy. As it pours out, it counteracts the gravitational energy and the falling protons begin to slow down until the two forces are exactly balanced. At that point we have a stable cloud of hydrogen atoms being fused together into helium and pouring out a great quantity of energy. What do we call such a thing?

We call it a star.

This, in fact, is what most stars are: gravitationally bound bundles of hydrogen being fused into helium, producing energy that will last for millions or billions of years, depending on the size of the star. And so the process by which helium is synthesized from hydrogen inside a star is called *stellar nucleosynthesis.*

3. This is not the whole story, for if it were, we would live in a universe composed only of hydrogen and helium. It turns out that 99 percent of the universe we see is in fact composed of just those two elements, so we ought to be rather satisfied with a theory that explains them. Since, however, we live on a planet composed of such elements as oxygen, silicon, magnesium, aluminum, and iron and since we live in bodies composed of carbon, nitrogen, oxygen, phosphorus, and hydrogen, we do feel compelled to find a theory that will explain the existence of these more complicated elements.

But before we push on theoretically, we should pause at this stage to once again ask the question, how do we know all this is true? We haven't, after all, traveled to any stars, so how do we know what they are made of? How do we know what provides their energy? It is time to remember the basic principle of science, testability: What observations do we have to confirm what we are thinking about?

It turns out that several lines of observation confirm our theory, and will in turn lead us on to the further knowledge that we seek. All of these observations rest on the light that comes from stars, so let's return to the subject of light, which we last left with Einstein.

FIFTEEN

The
Origin of Light

I. SO MUCH OF OUR THEORETICAL KNOWLEDGE OF THE
universe began with Einstein's quest to understand the nature of light,
and yet Einstein himself never did understand it, nor do we yet. He
found that he had to accept the fact that light travels at a constant
velocity, and from that he went on to understand many other things
about the universe, but the nature of light itself continued to elude him.
It is still a mystery to us, but we don't have to understand it to use it.

What is important to us in this section is not the nature of light, but
its origin; and we can understand the latter without the former, just as
we can understand how babies are born without understanding the
basic nature of humanity or human consciousness.

2. Electrons travel around the nuclei of atoms in well-constrained
orbits. When an atom is heated, the electrons absorb this energy by
bouncing up into higher orbits, whereupon they fall back again and
release the absorbed energy in the form of light.

This is, for example, how an electric light bulb works. We have a thin
wire, the filament, through which an electric current is passed, heating
it by friction as the electrons push through the wire. The atoms in the
wire are thus heated, and the electrons in the atoms jump up to higher
orbits; as they fall back again they emit light. (The glass bulb around the
wire is only to keep it sealed away from the oxygen in the air, which at
such a high temperature would oxidize it and burn it out rapidly. It is
because some oxygen gets in that the wire does eventually burn out.)

The particular wavelength of the light emitted is determined by the
distance between each two orbits that constitute the beginning and end
of each electron's jump. The orbital distances are different for each
different kind of atom—and so each different kind of atom (each ele-

ment) emits light of different series of wavelengths.

It is possible, therefore, to identify the atoms that are giving out light. Our eyes are not sensitive enough to do this, but we can build *optical spectrometers* to measure accurately the wavelength of light coming from any source, and thus we can tell if a light bulb has a copper filament or one made of another element.

When we look at the stars, we see the typical wavelengths of hydrogen and helium. In fact, when this was first done, helium had not yet been discovered. The first scientists to look at the sun's light in this way found that most of the light corresponded to the hydrogen wavelengths, but about 10 percent came at wavelengths that did not correspond to any known element. They were able to prove it came from a new element, which they named helium for the Greek god of the sun, Helios.

We have looked at the light from stars in all corners of the universe, both in our own galaxy and in far-off galaxies, and always the result is the same: Most of the light is from hydrogen, with a small percentage from helium, and only trace amounts from other elements.

So the first line of evidence is convincing. The stars are composed mostly of hydrogen and helium, as our theory says they should be. We find, however, one slight problem: The "other elements" mentioned above are composed of more complex atoms, such as oxygen, carbon, iron, and others. Where did these elements come from?

3. Aside from telling us the composition of the heated material, the light from a star can tell us two more things. First, a bigger fire will naturally give off a brighter light than will a smaller fire, so the brightness of a star tells us how big it is.[1] Second, we mentioned before that when you turn on the electric stove, its iron coil begins to glow dull red; if the temperature were raised, it would shine orange, then yellow, and finally would be white hot. So the *color* of the light emitted tells us how hot the object is, and this works for a star just as well as for a stove.

If we were to measure the color and brightness of a large number of stars, what would our theory tell us to expect?

Since clouds of hydrogen of any size might form,[2] we would expect

[1]This has to be corrected for distance, since a brighter faraway star can look dimmer than a smaller close star.
[2]There is actually a minimum size below which the total gravity would not be sufficient to pull the cloud together, but a wide variety of stars larger than this are allowed.

there to be stars of a wide range of sizes, and therefore a wide range of brightnesses. But the biggest stars should burn the hottest, just as on earth a whole wooden building on fire is hotter than just a couple of logs in a fireplace, though they are both of the same burning material. So we would expect a relationship between our two observables: Bright stars should be white, while dimmer stars should be red. Big stars, in other words, should be hot, and small stars cooler.

In fact, when we look at the stars, for most of them this is precisely what we see.

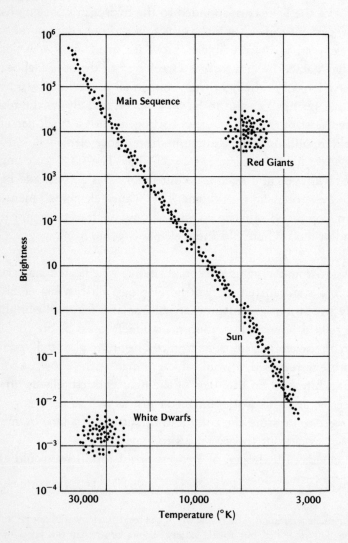

This diagram is called the Hertzsprung-Russell diagram, after the two astronomers who discovered the relationship. It shows that most stars lie on the main sequence, showing a direct proportionality between color and intensity, which translates into the expected correlation between mass and temperature of the stars. It is a beautiful confirmation of our theory.

But the observations go further: In the upper right-hand corner is a small group of large, cool stars, which we call Red Giants, and in the lower left corner is a group of small, hot stars, which we call White Dwarfs.

Our theory is going to have to explain those.

4. It should come as no surprise that the theory is as yet incomplete. It tells us how a star forms and how it provides energy to burn for millions or billions of years, depending on its mass. But millions and even billions of years, though a long time, are by no means forever. The universe has existed for *many* billions of years, and so our theory tells us that many stars must have already come to the end of their lifetime. What happens then? How does a star burn out, and what does a burnt-out star look like?

SIXTEEN

Stellar Nucleosynthesis B:
Helium to Iron: Red Giants and White Dwarfs

I. OUR THEORY TELLS US THAT A CLOUD OF HYDRO-
gen and helium condenses under the effect of its own gravity, leading
to high-energy collisions between hydrogen nuclei at the center. These
result in the fusion of hydrogen into helium, with a release of mass
energy as well, since the final helium weighs less than the initial hydrogen.

But the helium atoms in that original cloud must also be colliding with
each other and with hydrogen nuclei. What effect does this have on the
star?

None. Why? Because the helium nucleus consists of two protons and
two neutrons. Each of the two protons repels whatever protons or
helium nuclei it collides with, just as each proton repels every other
proton with its electromagnetic force. We have pointed out that at the
center of the star the protons are falling with enough gravitational
energy to overcome that repulsive force and thus to fuse into helium.
But the helium nuclei have *two* protons and thus twice as much repulsive force to be overcome.

In fact, it's even worse than that. The original helium-4 nuclei cannot
fuse with a proton anyway, for the same reason that nucleosynthesis in
the Big Bang stopped at mass four; no nucleus of mass five exists. They
can't fuse with each other for a double reason: Since they each have a
double charge, they would need *four* times the gravitational energy to
overcome that repulsive force; and also no nucleus of mass eight exists
for them to fuse into.

So, all in all, when the star forms, its energy source is the fusion of
hydrogen to helium; the helium itself contributes nothing. Now that
we've got that out of the way, let's continue with the life story of the
star.

2.   Eventually, all the helium that is being produced is going to get in the way, just as the ash of a burning fire will eventually put it out.

In a normal fire something like wood is burning. The burnt wood, the ash, consists of stuff that will not burn. As it is produced, it piles up around the fire and—if not removed—will shut out the oxygen and smother the fire.

In the star the helium is something similar. It doesn't "burn" because of its double repulsive force and because of the lack of anything to burn to at masses five and eight. But it's *there*, and as the protons bounce around, increasing numbers of them hit the helium nuclei. The collisions are wasted, with nothing in the sense of energy production being gained. Eventually so much helium accumulates that most of the protons are hitting helium atoms instead of each other. You can think of the situation as each proton being surrounded by heliums, so that it can't get through to find another proton with which to fuse. The helium is smothering the nuclear fire, just as ash smothers a wood fire.

So the fire dies out. What happens then?

3.   The main sequence star had a balance between two forces: Gravity was pulling it inward, and the nuclear fire was pushing it outward. Now the nuclear fire dies down, but the gravity doesn't. So what happens?

Right. The star begins to collapse again. It gets smaller, and the protons and helium nuclei bounce together with even more energy as they are squeezed tighter and tighter by the newly released gravitational energy. Are we on our way to producing a white dwarf?

Not exactly. Because eventually the helium atoms are bouncing together with so much energy that they can penetrate the electromagnetic barrier and begin to fuse together. No nucleus exists at mass eight, so two of them can't do anything, but what if *three* of them should come together? Then they could form a nucleus of mass twelve, and such a nucleus does indeed exist. It will have six protons and six neutrons (from the three helium nuclei), and this is a nucleus of the carbon-12 atom.

Furthermore, the carbon-12 atom weighs just a bit less than the three helium-4 atoms, so once again we have a release of mass-energy. The collapsing star once again has a nuclear fire at its center, and so its gravitational collapse is stabilized again. The nuclear fire this time is even hotter than in the main sequence stage—it has to be, in order to fuse the helium nuclei—and so the star swells up again. (This swelling effect can be seen easily with a balloon. Blow it up and tie off the cord. Put it in an oven at a low temperature and very quickly you will see it swell up. As the temperature in the oven increases, in fact, it will quickly swell so big that it will burst. If you catch it before it does, you can test the opposite effect by putting it in the refrigerator and watching it shrink. The whole effect is simply due to the nature of heat and of gases, which are composed of free atoms (or molecules) moving back and forth in random motion. Hotter atoms are atoms with more energy, moving faster and exerting more pressure on their surroundings. In the center of the star they are moving fast enough to fuse together, while in the balloon which is in the oven they are moving fast enough to push the sides of the balloon outward.)

At any rate, our new star, which began by shrinking and getting hotter, now becomes bigger—and cooler. At the center, where the helium is fusing, it's still hotter than the main sequence star it came from, but the outside of the star is now so far from the hot center that it cools off. (You can test this effect by simply holding your hand near a burning light bulb and then moving it closer. The closer you get, the more heat you feel; the farther away, the less.)

When we look at a star, we see only the outside, so what do we see when we look at this new star? It's big, so we see a giant. And its surface is cooler than it used to be, so its color has become red. We are looking at a red giant.

4. The basic energy source for the red giant is the fusion of three helium atoms into one carbon, and with this reaction we have the beginning of the reactions that have furnished the universe with the rich abundance of elements necessary for our planets and our life. In fact, what happens inside the red giant is a sequence of such reactions, repeated over and over again. Not only does the helium turn into carbon, but also other helium atoms now can fuse with the carbon in the same sort of reaction. This will produce an atom of eight protons and eight neutrons (six of each from the carbon, two of each from the helium), and this is an atom of oxygen-16. Further reactions produce neon-20, magnesium-24, silicon-28, and so on. And each of the new

86

nuclei have less mass than do the ones that formed it, so each reaction produces energy to keep the red giant burning.

Since it has roughly the same mass as the main sequence star it came from but is burning at a much higher temperature, it will run through its fuel much faster. A star the mass of the sun will last about ten billion years on the main sequence but only another few million years as a red giant. What happens next?

5. Again, it will collapse as its nuclear fuel is used up and the supporting nuclear fire goes out. This time, as it collapses, its future will depend on its mass. Let's first consider stars the size of the sun or a bit smaller.

Such a star will collapse with no more fuel to arrest its shrinkage. As it falls together, the nuclei bounce around and begin to smash each other to pieces, and the pieces—free protons and neutrons—smash into other nuclei and fuse with them. Some of the reactions produce more energy, but most of them actually suck up energy, thus hastening the collapse. These reactions will form other nuclei roughly up to the mass of iron, which is the most stable element. Above this level of about twenty-six protons and a few more neutrons, the nuclear production quickly dies out.

Eventually all the nuclei have fallen to the bottom, and when there is no more space into which to fall, the whole mess comes slowly to a stop.

What do we have then? A small star, surely. And a cold one? No, because in its helter-skelter falling together, all its gravitational energy has been released, and this has heated it up to a white heat. No further reactions take place to sustain the heat, and slowly it will cool off, but for the moment it is a small, white-hot star: a white dwarf.

Which means that our theory has now accounted for all the stars plotted on the Hertzsprung-Russell diagram and for the elements as massive as iron. That is pretty good, since it includes all the most important atoms for our planets and our bodies. But *all* the elements are important, not least of all simply because they exist, and our theory must account for them. And though we have explained everything plotted on the H-R diagram, this is not in fact everything in the universe.

There are, for example, sporadic but exciting things like supernovae.

These are suddenly appearing new stars, which come out of nowhere and flare up into the brightest stars in the skies for a few weeks or a few months and then disappear again.

What could they possibly be?

SEVENTEEN

Stellar Nucleosynthesis C:
Supernovae and the Rest
of the Elements

I. WHEN A MASSIVE STAR, ROUGHLY TEN TIMES BIGGER than the sun, runs out of its helium fuel, something similar yet different happens. Since it has run out of fuel, it must collapse, just as the smaller stars do; but since it is so much more massive, the collapse has a totally different effect.

There is so much gravitational energy released that the collapse runs away to the point of *implosion*. This is a word that denotes the opposite of an explosion; in the latter, as in a bomb explosion, everything goes flying out with enormous energy, while in the former everything comes flying inward.

It all comes flying in with such force that when all the particles meet at the center, as they must, they collide and rebound in a subsequent explosion. There are two results. One is that the central mass of the star, which has taken the full brunt of the imploding outer material, is crushed beyond recognition. The other is that the rebounding outer material goes flying out into space.

What we see when we look at such a situation is an exploding star, a supernova. One such star was noted by Chinese astronomers in 1054; what they saw was that in an apparently normal region of space, with many apparently normal stars in it, one star suddenly flared up and within a few weeks became as bright as the full moon; in another few weeks it had faded and disappeared. (It's interesting that no one in Europe saw this star. They must have, of course, but in 1054 the Church still had its hold on men's minds, and so everyone was convinced that the heavens were perfect and eternal—and therefore new stars *couldn't* suddenly appear, whether they were seen to do so or not. Therefore anyone who said they had seen such a thing would be a heretic, so apparently no one saw it.)

The Crab Nebula

When today we look at the region of space where the supernova appeared in 1054, we see the Crab Nebula. This is a vague cloud of expanding gases, lit by the remains of a star at its center. It's a perfect example of what must happen to a supernova after it dies away.

In terms of the nuclei of atoms, the supernova is interesting for another reason: It provides the synthesis of the heaviest elements, all the way up to uranium—and indeed beyond.

2. During the tremendous energy release of both the implosion and explosion phases, something different happens. As the nuclei crash together, they break each other apart, releasing tremendous numbers of neutrons and protons. The protons aren't able to fuse with most of the heavy elements that had already been formed (up to roughly the mass of iron), because these elements have a large number of protons in their nuclei and so the electromagnetic repulsion is too great for the protons to penetrate. The neutrons, however, are not affected by the electromagnetic force, they see no repulsive barrier, and so they slide right into these elements, forming new isotopes. So many of these neutrons suddenly flash around in the exploding star that a single nucleus might absorb many of them. An iron-56 nucleus, for example, might pick up a dozen neutrons to form the isotope iron-68.

It is a rough but firm law that in order for a nucleus to be stable, it must have approximately the same number of neutrons and protons, usually with a slight overabundance of neutrons. This is a rough law— for example, helium has two stable isotopes with one or two neutrons to balance its two protons, and oxygen has three stable isotopes with eight, nine, and ten neutrons for its eight protons—but it is a firm law. If a nucleus has too many or too few neutrons, it becomes radioactive.

The stable isotopes of iron are iron-54, -56, -57, and -58, with respectively 28, 30, 31, and 32 neutrons to balance its 26 protons. Iron-68 would be far overbalanced and must be radioactive.

There are two main types of radioactivity, called *alpha* and *beta*, after the first two letters of the Greek alphabet, to remind us of the origins of our science in Greece more than two thousand years ago. We are talking here about beta radioactivity, which is itself of two kinds: If a nucleus has too many protons for its neutrons, one proton will change into a neutron; if it has too many neutrons, the opposite will occur.

Iron-68 has 42 neutrons, many too many for its 26 protons, and so it will go through several radioactive decays, in each case one neutron changing to a proton and releasing an electron:

$$n \rightarrow p^+ + e^-$$

The electron goes flying out of the nucleus, and the proton remains in the new nucleus, replacing the neutron and changing the isotope into a new element with one higher proton number. The atom of iron-68 is now cobalt-68, with 27 protons and 41 neutrons. This is still too neutron rich, and so the process will occur again and again until it reaches the stable nucleus zinc-68, with 30 protons and 38 neutrons. It is these flying electrons, carrying away excess energy, that make radioactivity so unhealthy; if they hit you they can knock apart your molecules, leading to radiation sickness, cancer, and death.

This process is called the *rapid* neutron-capture process, since a single nucleus can capture many neutrons so rapidly that it doesn't have a chance to undergo radioactive decay between captures; then after the capture process is over, the nucleus decays consecutively to a stable species. In contrast, the *slow* neutron-capture process allows radioactive decay to take place in between successive neutron captures; this process has been taking place during the red-giant phase previous to the supernova explosion.

In the red giant, accompanying the fusion processes that build carbon, oxygen, neon, and other elements by adding helium nuclei together, are other reactions in which the helium additions are incomplete, splitting off free neutrons. These neutrons float through the red giant and often find another nucleus to slip into. Thus an oxygen-16 nucleus might capture a neutron to form oxygen-17, but this is also a stable isotope and will not decay. Eventually it might capture another neutron to form oxygen-18, and this, too, is stable; but if it captures one more, it will finally have too many neutrons for stability and the resulting oxygen-19 (eight protons and eleven neutrons) will decay to fluorine-19 (nine protons and ten neutrons).

The stable fluorine-19 may eventually capture another neutron to form fluorine-20, which will then decay to neon-20. This slow neutron-capture process can continue, forming elements as massive as bismuth-209, but there it must stop because all elements heavier than bismuth are *alpha*-radioactive. These decay by emitting alpha particles, which are actually helium nuclei: two protons and two neutrons bound together by the strong nuclear force. This turns the bismuth, with 82 protons, into an isotope of the lighter element thallium, with 80 protons, so that the process cannot form any heavier elements.

But if an atom of bismuth, in the supernova event, captures a large number of neutrons—for example, twenty-nine of them—it would form bismuth-238. This isotope is so neutron-to-proton-rich that instead of decaying by alpha emission, it would undergo beta decay, changing step by step into other elements and ending up as uranium-238, the most common isotope of uranium.

Uranium actually has no stable isotopes, but it exists on earth because uranium-238 has a half-life of about four and a half billion years. That means that it takes that long for half the uranium originally formed to disappear. Since the earth is four and a half billion years old, half the uranium that was originally here is still with us.

Other atoms even heavier than uranium can be built in the rapid capture process of a supernova; uranium is in no way special. But all the heavier elements, things like plutonium and californium, are radioactive with half-lives much shorter than the age of the solar system; therefore all those isotopes have alpha-decayed back into lighter elements long ago and are no longer present on earth.

Eventually the uranium, too, will all disappear by radioactivity, but long before it does, we ourselves will have disappeared when our main sequence sun enters its red-giant stage.

When this happens, the sun will first cool and shrink as its hydrogen furnace is turned off, and we will all freeze to death, our oceans turned into solid ice. Then, as the helium furnace turns on, the sun will heat up and the oceans will boil; finally the sun will expand and totally envelope the earth.

The poet Robert Frost has speculated that "some say the world will end in fire, / some say in ice." We can say with certainty that it will end in both, first freezing and then burning. But we also know that won't happen until the sun reaches the end of its main sequence stage, and since we understand pretty well how the nuclear fire burns and we know pretty exactly the mass of the sun and when it was created, four and a half billion years ago, we can predict that it won't happen for roughly another five billion years or so.

And with luck, we'll be long gone from this earth by then, able to travel throughout the galaxy. We'd *better* be.

EIGHTEEN
Pulsars

I. SO FAR, WE HAVE CREATED ALL THE ELEMENTS OF which the universe is composed, and we have discussed the life and death of stars from their beginnings through the main sequence to the red-giant stage and on to their death as white dwarfs or supernovae, but we haven't actually finished with the supernovae. The outer parts of the star explode, but remember the inner core? What happens to that?

Let's consider a star about ten times more massive than the sun. When it implodes, the inner core is compressed to a state denser than anything we know on earth. The core is squeezed so tightly together that the force of gravity overcomes all other forces, breaking apart the structure of the atoms and pulling the electrons right into the nuclei. There they combine with the positive protons to form neutrons (the process is the opposite of the beta decay of neutrons), and so the entire star becomes simply a gigantic ball of neutrons.

When this possibility was discussed theoretically, in the first half of this century, it was named a neutron star. The mathematics that described it seemed reasonable, but the next step seemed impossible: The next step would be, of course, to look out into the universe and see if such neutron stars exist. But what would they look like?

They would be very small and very hot, but no one was able to predict anything particularly different about such a star; no one could tell what it would look like or if in fact it would look any different from any other small, hot star.

And then, in 1967, one particular star began to wink at a young woman named Jocelyn Bell.

Miss Bell (now Mrs. Burnell) was a graduate student in radio astronomy at Cambridge University, in England (where Newton had studied). Radio astronomy is a branch of the science that studies stars, not by the visible light they emit, but by their radio waves. This is not to suggest that there are star-people broadcasting radio programs to us, but that all hot objects emit electromagnetic radiation at a variety of wavelengths. The entire electromagnetic spectrum runs from very high-energy, short-wavelength gamma rays and X rays, through ultraviolet light to visible light, and on into the infrared and, with the longest wavelengths of all, radio waves. The spectrum can be illustrated like this:

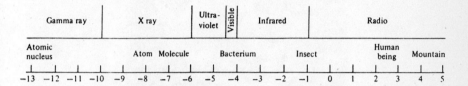

In this diagram the wavelengths are written as 10^{-X}, so that X rays have wavelengths of about 10^{-8} cm, and radio waves are greater than 10^{-1} cm. For comparison purposes some familiar objects are listed: an atomic nucleus has a size of about 10^{-13} cm, and a mountain is about 10^4 cm high.

Our sun emits most of its energy in the visible region, but it—and all other stars—emit some radiation in all regions of the spectrum. The science of radio astronomy made its first public impression during the Second World War, when radar operators in England received a sudden burst of activity on their sets. Thinking that it was a massive raid by Germany, they launched all their fighters, but there were no German bombers in the air at all. When the same radar signal came in for several days in a row, the scientists who had become worried about it noticed that the signal came always from the east at dawn. It was not German bombers whose signals the radar sets had picked up, they realized, but the rising sun, which had sprouted what is called a radio storm. After the war, these scientists started building radio receptors specifically designed to measure the radio waves coming from the sun and from other stars. They found that some stars, known as radio stars, emit most of their energy in the radio wave region.

Jocelyn Bell was engaged in making a radio map of such stars. She had built her own radio telescope, as it is called, and was making a survey of faint radio stars when she noticed one particular star that appeared

95

Dr. Jocelyn Bell
Burnell

to be winking at her. That is, it was giving off short bursts of energy very rapidly and very regularly. The bursts were terribly short, lasting less than one hundredth of a second, and they repeated themselves at the remarkably precise interval of every 1.3373013 second.

She reported this to her faculty adviser, Anthony Hewish, who told her that such behavior was impossible. Stars do not turn on and off like that; there were good mathematical reasons why they could not possibly do so. The cause must be some fault in the radio telescope.

Why was such stellar behavior impossible? First of all, if an object emits energy, it has to be spread out and received on earth at different times because of the size of the emitting object, which blurs the precision of the signal. The larger the emitting object, the greater the blurring. Hewish and Bell could easily calculate that signals received in bursts lasting less than 0.01 second indicated an emitting object less than ten miles in radius.

That was impossible. The sun, a typical small star, is nearly a half-million miles in radius. White dwarfs, the smallest known stars, are about ten thousand miles in radius. A star less than ten miles in radius was simply too small to exist. (It would not be massive enough to initiate the hydrogen burning and so would never turn into a star at all.)

96

Second, the repetition rate of the bursts, every 1.3373013 seconds, was much more regular than any natural process. When one is confronted with two such seeming impossibilities, the most likely explanation is a fault in the apparatus. So Jo Bell was sent back to find the problem in her equipment.

She didn't find one. Instead she found that no matter how hard she checked out her telescope, that damned star was still winking at her.

The people at her lab began to think that the signals were real, but what could they be? Perhaps, they thought, the signals were from an extraterrestrial civilization. The small size might indicate a spaceship, and the signals were coming from someone out there shouting hello to the galaxy and hoping for some answer. They began to refer to the signals as LGMs, taking the term from science fiction, where it is used as an acronym for Little Green Men, the kind of beings people used to imagine lived on Mars.

Continuing her work, Jo Bell discovered another LGM, and then another. Other workers in the lab now found still more. They had probably been discovered earlier but had been dismissed without thought as an experimental problem of no importance. Now suddenly the sky was full of these winking radio stars, which meant that they couldn't be little green men at all. The galaxy couldn't be full of such civilizations, or contact would have been made before.

The answer to the problem came from Tommy Gold, an astrophysicist then at Cornell University. His solution was just as radical as the LGM explanation and at first was received no more seriously. When he tried to present his idea at a scientific meeting, he was told that they didn't have time for such speculation. ("Speculation" is a fairly polite way scientists have of referring to what they really consider to be nonsense). However, when people finally listened to him, they were soon convinced that he was right.

The winking stars, Gold suggested, were actually the long-sought neutron stars. He argued that the *pulsars*, as they were now called, were extremely small, less than ten miles in radius, as a consequence of being an imploded state of neutron matter, with the core of nearly an entire normal star squeezed into a small inner sphere. He went on to explain their pulsating radio emissions as a sort of searchlight effect.

He showed that such a neutron star would have to have a particularly intense magnetic field surrounding it. (Stars and most planets do have such magnetic fields associated with them. That's what gives us the north and south magnetic poles on earth and allows compasses to work.) The effect of the postulated implosion would be to compress the star's normal magnetic field into a small but very intense one; it would, in fact, be so intense that it would focus the star's outgoing radiation at two opposite points on its surface. The other effect of importance would be due to the conservation of angular momentum.

Conservation is a term in science that means that the stuff conserved can be neither created nor destroyed. There are many conservation laws, and they are of tremendous help in analyzing different situations. One that is particularly obvious to us is the conservation of mass: Mass is neither created nor destroyed.[1] What a queer universe this would be if mass could sometimes appear or disappear without a trace.

It turns out that angular momentum is also conserved. This concept arises in any case of an object in curved motion. Consider a stone whirled around in a circle. The stone's angular momentum is its mass times its velocity times its distance from the center, $m \times v \times r$. Any star spinning on its axis will have a certain amount of angular momentum, which must be conserved. If the star implodes, everything gets closer to the center; the factor r gets smaller. Since its mass remains the same (as long as the velocity is nowhere near the speed of light), the only way for the product mvr to remain constant is if the velocity v gets bigger, and that is what must happen. So the imploded core of a star, the neutron star, must be spinning very fast.

The combination of this rapid spinning and intense magnetic focusing of radiation gives the neutron star a lighthouse effect; it sends out its radiation in a narrow, spinning beam, just as a lighthouse does. We see such a star only when it comes around and points directly at us, and then we see it as a quick blink of energy, just as we see the lighthouse beam only when it whirls around and points at us.

To confirm this idea, people looked at the center of the Crab Nebula. This is the remnant of the 1054 supernova, and so—if Gold was right—there should have been a neutron star left behind at its center. People had of course studied the Crab before, but not knowing what to look

---

[1]This was modified by Einstein so that it is now called the conservation of mass-energy, since mass can be changed into an equivalent amount of energy or vice versa.

for, they hadn't found anything. Now when they looked, they saw indeed a pulsar right there at the center.

This story of the discovery of neutron stars—which incidentally resulted in a Nobel Prize for Anthony Hewish, but not for Jocelyn Bell or Tommy Gold—just about brings to a close our description of the different kinds of stars in our universe. Just about, but not quite. We've saved the best for last, and now we'll talk about . . .

Black holes. . . .

NINETEEN
Black Holes

I. THE CONCEPT OF BLACK HOLES, LIKE THAT OF NEU-
tron stars, first arose theoretically. Shortly after Einstein published the
relativistic theory of gravity, a German colleague, Karl Schwarzschild,
began to wonder what would happen if the curvature of a small region
of space became infinite.

How could that happen? Consider the surface of a star, and in our
gedankenexperiment let's make the star cool enough for a man to stand
on. The force of gravity he feels is determined accurately enough by
Newton's equation, $F = GmM/d^2$, where m is the man's mass and M
is the star's mass, and d is the distance from him to the center of the
star (the radius of the star).

Now suppose the star, without changing its mass, begins to shrink.
The distance d gets smaller, so the force of gravity F gets bigger. In
Einstein's view, the curvature of space around the surface of the star gets
greater. Suppose the star continues to shrink: the curvature gets greater
and greater until it becomes infinite.

What does this mean? It means that nothing would have enough
energy to escape from the gravitational field of the star, not even a beam
of light. If our hypothetical person were to try to signal to a passing
spaceship with a flashlight, the beam of light would bend over and curve
right back down again to the surface of the star; the spaceship would
pass by and never would see the beam.[1]

The light of the star would behave in the same way. If it were hot and
shining like a normal star, no one would ever see it because its light

---

[1] Of course this wouldn't worry our man on the star. He would be crushed out of
existence by the tremendous gravity and wouldn't be worrying about anything.

would bend over and fall back to its surface. Anything that approached it would be sucked in by that gravity and would never be able to emerge again.

Such a hypothetical object was named a "black hole" after the infamous nineteenth-century prison in Calcutta from which, it was said, a prisoner once incarcerated never emerged again. In the early years of this century Schwarzchild's stellar black holes were thought to be interesting but hardly relevant to reality, for how could a star shrink like that?

But with our new theories of the life and death of stars, the possibility became apparent. If a truly massive star, say, one a hundred times larger than the sun, were to evolve into a red giant and then a supernova, it would—when it imploded—have sufficient gravity because of its large mass to compress the inner core beyond the neutron star stage into a black hole.

Or so people thought. But how could they prove it? The only way would be to observe a black hole, and how can you see something that is by definition invisible?

2. H. G. Wells once wrote a novel called *The Invisible Man,* later made into a fine film with Claude Rains. It concerns a man made invisible and the efforts by the authorities to find him. How could that be done?

Suppose such an invisible man were standing by the side of the road and a passing car splashed mud on him. Then, although you couldn't see the man, you could see the mud sticking to him. Or if he came pushing through a crowd of people, you could follow his progress by the commotion he made. If he were swimming, you could see his wake in the water.

In other words, you could see the invisible man by his interactions with the rest of the universe.

3. In 1970 NASA sent off a satellite named *Uhuru.* Its purpose was to extend our observations of the universe beyond the visible and radio regions of the electromagnetic spectrum by looking for X rays. The reasoning was that stars should emit energy in all regions of the spectrum, and perhaps if we looked in a new region we might find something new.

101

We certainly did. *Uhuru* found a stellar source of X rays in the constellation of Cygnus, the Swan, and so the source was named Cyg X-1. The source was pulsating, and its periodicity was short enough to indicate an object smaller than a white dwarf. But the mass of the source, as calculated from the intensity of the X rays, turned out to be much greater than that of a white dwarf or even a neutron star, and no trace of a supernova explosion was found. In fact, when the astronomers looked for Cyg X-1 in visible light, they found a binary star with an invisible twin.

Binary stars are common features of the universe. We have mentioned how stars form by condensing out of a cloud of hydrogen and helium. It turns out that the condensation process often results in two stars rather than one; something like half the stars in the galaxy are such binary stars.

Two stars, formed in close proximity to each other, will be bound in each other's gravitational fields and so will revolve around each other. One star is often much more massive than the other, and so the observed effect is that the smaller star is seen to be revolving around the larger.

But when the astronomers looked at Cyg X-1 they saw just one star, revolving around *nothing*. Clearly that was impossible; the only way to make a star move in a circular path is to have a heavier star at the center of the circle, holding the revolving star in its gravity, just as our sun holds the planets. But try as hard as they could, they could find no star in the center of the circle around which the visible star moved.

When they aligned the X ray observations carefully with the visual observations, they found a slight discrepancy: The light from the star wasn't coming from exactly the same place the X rays were coming from! Careful measurements established the fact that the X rays were coming from the center of the circle around which the star was moving—from the *empty* center of the circle.

Putting it all together, what they had was a star gravitationally bound to an invisible central star that was emitting X rays, a star that had to be more massive than the visible star, which was itself rather large. The explanation that was finally arrived at goes like this: A binary pair of stars forms, one of which is much heavier than the other. Being more massive, it burns through its main sequence stage more quickly, goes through its red-giant phase, and explodes as a supernova. The inner core, being so immense, is compressed into a black hole. The visible star remains today in orbit around its companion, which we can no longer see. The tremendous gravity of the black hole is continually sucking material off the surface of its companion. As the material swirls down onto the black hole, it falls faster and faster, actually reaching the speed of light just as it crosses the gravitational boundary into the black hole itself. This acceleration causes the falling material to leave the universe with a heart-rending death scream in the form of an emitted stream of X rays, so that we see them coming from what looks like the empty center of the star's orbit but is actually the surface of the black hole.

I say the material leaves the universe, because once it falls into the black hole it can never come out again, and so for all practical purposes it has left our universe. There might even be a deeper meaning there. Inside a black hole conditions are so intense that they approximate a singularity; a black hole has been described as a star that has been crushed out of existence, leaving behind only an empty hole in space-time. Obviously we are again running up against the limits of our knowledge; we don't understand what happens inside a black hole.

But there are some interesting suggestions. One is that black holes might be passageways into other universes or other domains of our own universe, with each black hole where matter disappears from our universe being matched with a "white hole," where matter *appears* into another universe. But if this were true, one would expect to find in our own universe such white holes—marked by the inexplicable appearance of matter out of seeming nothingness—which would be the reverse of black holes in another universe, and such white holes have never been found.

This fact—that white holes have not been found in our universe—is an indication that they don't exist in others. But not necessarily. Perhaps we don't know where to look in this vast universe, or don't know what to look for. After all, pulsars and black holes have existed forever but were only recently discovered, because scientists didn't know what to look for. They were found only accidentally. One of the few certainties in our uncertain future is that certainly a lot more accidental discoveries are waiting to be made.

On the other hand, the fact that something hasn't been observed certainly can't be taken as evidence that it *does* exist. Everything that we imagine doesn't turn out to be true. The planet Vulcan, for example, was never found, because it doesn't exist; the explanation for Mercury's orbital motion was found to be something quite different.

I mention white holes mainly as another reminder of all the things that we still don't know. Maybe they exist, maybe not. The science that you are taught in school very properly concentrates on teaching what we know; a main purpose of this book is to remind you of what we *don't* know, of what is out there waiting to be discovered. Who knows what the future may bring?

In the meanwhile, a more realistic and hardly less dramatic story is the possible explanation of quasars as gigantic black holes in the act of swallowing whole galaxies.

4. *Quasar* is the short name given to quasi-stellar objects: things that look like stars but can't be.[1] They can't be because, although they are roughly star-sized, they shine with the light of an entire galaxy, about a hundred billion times brighter than our sun. No known energy source is powerful enough to make our sun shine that brightly, hence the name. The most recent suggestion for such a source of energy comes from the observation that a quasar seems to be at the center of most old galaxies, and from the observed behavior of Cyg X-1.

What will happen to Cyg X-1 when it has swallowed up all the material of its companion star? It will have grown by all the mass it swallowed and if there were another star close by, it might then be massive enough to reach out and swallow it up. And it might again grow by what it feeds on and in time reach out farther and farther, swallowing stars more and more voraciously. And as it gets bigger, it could end up by swallowing stars whole, emitting tremendous bursts of radiation as they fall into its gaping maw, finally sucking up its whole galaxy and burning as brightly as the galaxy itself with the death gasps of the stars that will be falling into it every second.

It has been suggested, but not proved, that as galaxies form they do so with a large black hole at their center, and that as time goes on this

---

[1]The prefix *quasi* comes from two Latin words that, taken together, mean approximately "almost but not quite."

black hole swallows up the stars around it, slowly at first. But then, as it grows, it swallows them faster and faster and ends by consuming the entire galaxy. This might be the future in store for all stars of all galaxies, including our own, particularly since a recent observation seems to show such a black hole at the center of our own Milky Way galaxy.

Perhaps T. S. Elliot was right when he wrote:

"This is the way the world ends
Not with a bang but a whimper."

TWENTY
What If...?

I.   NOW THAT WE HAVE SEEN WHAT THINGS LOOK LIKE in this universe of ours, we can entertain ourselves by wondering what if they were just a little bit different. When we look at the Hertzsprung-Russell diagram, we see that the sun is a typical main sequence star—but there are such wide ranges of possible main sequence stars. The sun could easily be, for example, ten or a hundred or a thousand times bigger. What difference would that make to us?

If it were bigger, it would be hotter, of course. And that would mean that the earth would be too hot for life. But that's not necessarily tragic, because, as we will see in the next section, Mars is a planet very similar to earth, and it's roughly twice as far away from the sun, which means it gets only about one-quarter as much heat. So if the earth were too hot for life, perhaps Mars would take its place.

But, as we said earlier in the book, the bigger a star is, the more rapidly it burns its fuel. A star the size of the sun remains on the main sequence for about ten billion years, but larger stars will run through their hydrogen fuel at a much faster rate. A star more than ten times the mass of the sun will finish its main sequence stage in less than one billion years, and where would that leave us?

Life began on earth within the first billion years of its existence,[1] but nothing remotely resembling human consciousness evolved until within the last few million years. That means it took nearly four billion years for any creatures capable of conscious thought to evolve; in fact, it took nearly four billion years for anything much more complex than a jellyfish to evolve. All of the complex living creatures of this planet came into

[1]The earliest known fossils, of simple creatures like algae, are about 3.9 billion years old.

existence within only the last 600 million years; for the first 3.9 billion years of existence, this planet was home to only the most primitive forms of life.

Remember what will happen when the sun uses up its hydrogen fuel and moves on to the red-giant stage? It will cool down, and all the water on earth—and all living creatures great and small—will freeze to death. Then the sun will swell up and envelop the earth, and our frozen corpses will boil off into gas.

So if the sun were a larger star and had a lifetime of only a billion years or so, where would we be? In never-ever land, to put it euphemistically.

2. Or suppose the sun were a first-generation star, one of the first stars to condense after the creation of the universe in the Big Bang.

At that time the entire universe consisted of only hydrogen and helium, so of course that was what the first stars consisted of. And the planets?

They couldn't consist of anything else, because there *wasn't* anything else. The giant planets of our solar system (as we'll discuss in the next chapter) are composed almost entirely of these two elements, and so we know that it is possible to form such planets. But they are totally different from earth. Of even more importance, we shall see that any kind of life needs the element carbon, as well as a few others. But those first planets (if they existed) and those first stars had no carbon, only hydrogen and helium.

Where did the carbon come from? In those stars and in later ones it was formed when they passed through the red-giant stage. So couldn't life have been formed then?

Hardly. The carbon atoms, remember, are formed in the inside of the star, at temperatures of about 10^8 degrees (a hundred million degrees). This is hotter than Miami in August, and neither the red giant nor Miami in August is a fit place for living creatures. Specifically, life needs liquid water, and water boils into a gas at 100 degrees, so no life is going to be found inside stars.

Then how did the carbon on earth get here? Remember what happens after the red-giant phase: Stars blow up and scatter their material out into the universe. (Even stars that don't become supernovae go through a stage where their outer envelopes are blown off into space.) The heavy elements that were created in their various stages of development, including carbon and oxygen, iron and uranium, *all* of the elements, are blown off into space, where they spend a few eternities whirling around and mixing with all the primordial hydrogen and helium already out there. And when, eventually, the next cloud of hydrogen and helium begins to condense into a star, it includes some small amount of heavy elements that were once formed inside a now long-dead and disappeared star.

That is how our own sun formed. It is a *second-generation* star; the name doesn't pretend to mean that the sun is really only the second generation, but simply that it formed after the first generation, after heavy elements were manufactured and dispersed back into space, to be incorporated in our sun and planets. If the sun were first generation, it could not possibly have any form of life on any of its planets.

3. Finally, what if our sun were a binary star? We have mentioned that roughly half of all stars in the universe are, so our sun easily might have been one. What would have become of us then?

The answer is that it depends on the masses of the two stars. The difference between a star and a planet is that a star provides its own energy, with a nuclear furnace at its core, while a planet is dead, shining only by the reflected light of its parent star. The only thing that determines whether a body will form a nuclear furnace at its center is the amount of gravitational energy with which it can squeeze its atoms together. It must squeeze them together with enough energy to overcome the repulsive electromagnetic force, allowing them to fuse and liberate nuclear energy. The only thing that determines the amount of gravitational energy a body has is its mass. So a body big enough will become a star; one not big enough will become a planet.

In our own solar system, Jupiter is nearly big enough to be a star. If it had just a bit more mass, Jupiter could have turned on and then it and our sun would be a binary pair.

And that would not have affected us very much at all. Jupiter would be a lot brighter and the night sky a lot less dark, but Jupiter is much farther from us than is the sun, and it would not have been as bright a star as the sun anyway (being so much smaller than the sun). So earth still would have had night and day. Life would almost certainly have evolved in much the same way as it did.

On the other hand, if the solar system had formed with two stars of nearly the same mass, things could have been quite different. It would be hard to find a stable, nearly circular planetary orbit in such a system, because the planets would be pulled by both stars in such a manner as to give them eccentric swings.[2] If a planet's orbit is too eccentric, it will approach the star so close in summer that all its oceans will boil—as will the blood in any living creatures—while in winter it will recede so far away that all its oceans and blood will freeze. Planets in such orbits would not have the long-term temperature stability necessary for the development of life and so would probably remain barren.

4. In short, there is a wide range of possible ways stars may form but only a small number compatible with the formation of life, particularly of intelligent life. If any one of a number of things had been just a bit different, we never would have existed.

Does this mean once again that we are the center of the universe, in the sense that everything seems to have been created just right for us? As if a benevolent creator had taken care of things for our comfort?

Well, let's talk about the creation of our earth and see.

[2]Unless they are either very close to one star (and far from the other) or orbiting both stars at a great distance. In the former case the planet probably would be too close and therefore too hot for life; in the latter case it would be too far away and thus too cold.

PART III

THE
EARTH

TWENTY-ONE
The Solar System

1.   IT IS CLEAR BY NOW THAT THE EARTH IS SIMPLY ONE of a series of planets revolving around our sun. It occupies no particularly unique position; a visitor coming into our solar system would not immediately pick it out as the most important of the planets. It is neither the biggest nor the smallest, neither the closest to the sun nor the farthest away. Its orbit is neither the most circular nor the most elliptical. It is, in short, typical rather than unique. It would obviously be a mistake to try to figure out its origin as if it were one of a kind, rather than being one of a family of planets. In order to understand how the earth was created, we have to know how all the planets were created. In order to do this, we must first have a clear idea of what the family of planets looks like, what its characteristics are: What are the facts that must be explained by any theory of its origin?

2.   The sun constitutes 99.9 percent of the entire solar system, and this must be the first clue to its origin. Surely the family of planets is a small subsidiary to the sun, and the origin of planets cannot be considered as a problem separate from the existence of the sun. The planets could not have been created by themselves, with the sun later stuck into their center. We shall see, in fact, that we have today two possible theories of planetary origins; one of them—by far the favorite—supposes that the planets originated in the same process that formed the sun, while the other sees an accidental encounter between the sun and another star. But before we go into details, let's learn more about the sun and its family of planets.

First of all, the planets all revolve around the sun in the same direction and all nearly within the same plane (except for Pluto, the farthest planet). They all spin in the same direction as their orbital motion, except for Venus, which spins backward, and Uranus and Pluto, which are lying on their sides. Most of the moons of the planets, though not all, also orbit and spin in this same direction and plane.

Obviously this motion is not random nor by chance; it must be due to something basic about the formation of the system of planets and moons.

Next, if we list the size, density, mass, and number of moons of the planets in order of their distance from the sun, we see another aspect of the family:[1]

PLANET	Mass	Radius	Density	Moons
Mercury	0.056	0.38	0.98	0
Venus	0.81	0.95	0.93	0
Earth	1.00	1.00	1.00	1
Mars	0.11	0.53	0.72	2
Jupiter	318	11	0.23	16
Saturn	95	9.5	0.12	21
Uranus	15	4.1	0.21	15
Neptune	17	3.9	0.29	2
Pluto	0.002	0.25	0.36	1

First, ignore Pluto because we know so little about it, since it is so far away from us. Now the first four planets, the inner planets, are all the same mass and size of the earth, or smaller; they have pretty much the same density and basically have no moons.

(Okay, the earth and Mars have moons. But the martian moons are probably captured asteroids instead of being true moons, and so the earth is the only one of the group to have a moon. This moon is very bothersome; we'll talk about it later, after we've set up some background information.)

The outer planets, on the other hand, have lots of moons—except for Neptune, which probably has many more moons that we haven't discovered yet because the planet and its moons are so far away. These outer planets are different in other ways. They are suddenly much bigger than

[1]For simplicity, we give all values relative to the earth values.

the earth and at the same time have much smaller densities. Taking all these characteristics into account, we can break up the planets into two groups: The inner ones are earthlike, and are called the terrestrial planets, while the outer ones are giants, like Jupiter, and are called the major or giant or Jovian planets. (The change from Jupiter to Jovian arises from the peculiarities of the Latin language, with which you are no doubt familiar.)

This distinction continues if we look at the chemical characteristics of the planets:

Element	Sun	Terrestrial Planets	Jupiter
Hydrogen	94%	~0.1%	~84%
Helium	5	~0	~ 5
Oxygen	~1	50	~10
Silicon	~0	15	~ 0
Iron	~0	20	~ 0

All these values are approximate, but they illustrate the similarity of Jupiter to the sun and the difference between it and the terrestrial planets. Clearly we cannot say that all the planets are similar to each other, but we will have to account for these observed differences, which are also apparent if we take a close look at the individual planets.

Mercury, the closest to the sun, was almost impossible to see clearly until 1974, when our unmanned spaceship *Mariner 10* approached within 500 miles of the planet and took its picture. The first photo shows the best picture ever taken of the planet from earth: All you can see is a hazy ball. Contrast it with the next, taken by *Mariner 10* as it sailed by. We see a pockmarked surface very similar to the familiar one of our own moon. Conditions on the surface of Mercury are very different from those on the moon, however, because it is so close to the sun. The temperature rises to more than 500 degrees centigrade there in the day, dropping to −200 degrees at night. This extreme range of temperatures, the greatest in the solar system, is because Mercury has no atmosphere to absorb the sun's heat and hold it during the night; the normal atmospheric gases have been boiled away by the sun's heat. If you were to visit Mercury and put a bar of solid lead or zinc metal on the ground, it would melt when the sun's rays hit it, while at night gases like the

Mercury from
500 miles away.

Mercury close up

carbon dioxide that we all breathe out would freeze solid and drop to the ground.

Venus is much closer to us and is far enough from the sun not to be lost in its glare. It does remain close to the sun, as seen from earth, and so is always a morning or evening star, leading or trailing the sun in its journey and visible only just before dawn or just after sunset, but at those times it is brilliant—the brightest planet in the sky. This photo shows Venus as *Mariner 10* sped by on its way to Mercury. Instead of a pockmarked surface we see something like what earth looks like, a surface hidden behind a thick, blanketing atmosphere. Venus's atmosphere, however, is very different. On earth our carbon dioxide has been used by plants to form their bodies, and has been precipitated in the form of carbonate rocks or kept in solution in the oceans. On Venus the temperature is so hot that the carbon dioxide is all in the atmosphere, and this makes the atmosphere even hotter. This is because carbon dioxide is transparent to visible light, and so the sun's radiant energy penetrates it and heats the surface of the planet. It is reirradiated at longer wavelengths, toward which the carbon dioxide is *not* transparent. This long wavelength radiation is therefore trapped in the atmosphere and heats it up.

This mechanism provides an efficient heat trap, allowing some of the sun's heat to penetrate to the surface but not allowing it to be reirradiated back out to space; it is known as the greenhouse effect, because the glass walls of our greenhouses perform much the same function, which is why they can be so warm inside even in winter. Temperatures on Venus are over 400 degrees, night and day.

(Incidentally, Venus provides a warning to us on earth. We are burning our fossil fuels with abandon, and when burned they release carbon dioxide into the atmosphere. Our atmosphere is being enriched in this gas beyond natural levels, and if it continues, we face a real danger that the temperature of the earth will warm by a few degrees. If it does, the polar ice caps will begin to melt, with catastrophic consequences.

(At the present time we have a delicate balance of temperature effects on earth. The polar ice caps, for example, reflect a large amount of the sun's radiation out into space, keeping the earth cool. If the caps begin to melt, they will reflect less heat—since the melted ice, water, absorbs more of the heat, rather than reflecting it—and that will make the earth

Venus

even warmer. So once they begin to melt, the effect could become a runaway warming trend, which would then go on to melt the rest of the ice caps.

(If the caps should melt, they would add so much water to the oceans that sea level would rise by many feet. Miami, where I live today, is a few inches above sea level, so such an event would be disastrous. In fact, most of the major cities of the world—New York, San Francisco, London, Amsterdam—would be drowned, as would many of the fertile, food-producing areas. It would be a catastrophe unprecedented in human history.

(Right now we aren't quite sure how close we are to bringing this down on our heads. The carbon dioxide balance in and on our planet is a complicated one, involving the oceans and the forests as well as our fossil-fuel-burning budget, and we have to do a lot more research before we understand what we should be doing to alleviate the problem. Let's hope we get the research done in time.)

The third planet is earth, shown here. The chemical composition of all three of these planets is quite similar overall, although the histories since their birth have changed their configurations. For example, as we said, most of the carbon dioxide on Venus is in its atmosphere, while it has been lost from Mercury because of the sun's heat, and on earth it is tied up in biological compounds, in rocks, and in the oceans.

The fourth and last terrestrial planet is Mars. This photo shows the surface as seen by *Viking*, the spacecraft that we sent there in 1976 to look for life. It found a dry, rocky surface quite similar to that of earth with only a problematical hint of life.

The biggest difference among the four planets, as far as we are concerned, is the presence or absence of liquid water—since it, together with the element carbon, is the basic necessity for life. Mercury has no water at all because it is much too hot; the water that originally might have been there was quickly boiled to steam and—since the planet is so hot and so small, with little gravitational energy to hold the gaseous water molecules—they were evaporated away into space. Venus has lost most of its water, and since the greenhouse effect keeps the surface temperature at over 400 degrees centigrade, and the centigrade scale is defined with the boiling point of water at 100 degrees, there is no possibility of liquid water there.

Earth, of course, is just right, while Mars is too far away from the sun. The temperatures there are below the freezing point of water, 0 degrees centigrade, except for a few regions during bright and direct sunlight. At one time we had thought the martian polar cap was similar to our own, and when it melted in summer we had envisaged a torrent of water cascading over the martian surface, but now we have discovered that the martian cap is largely frozen carbon dioxide. However, we have also discovered what appear to be great dried-up river beds on Mars (see photo), indicating that at past times there may well have been significant amounts of water on the surface. By now this may have been evaporated

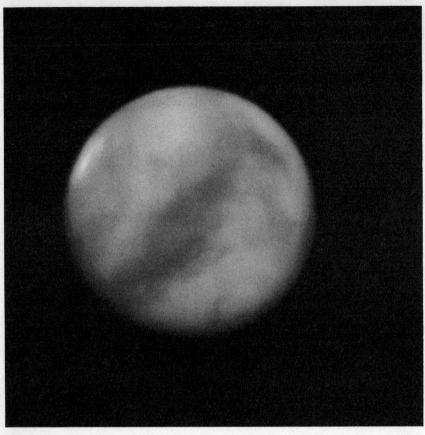

Mars

off into space, since Mars is smaller than the earth, or it may be frozen underground. For this reason, and because of the inconsistent experimental results returned by *Viking,* we're not quite sure whether life ever existed on Mars or not.[2]

3. Beyond Mars lies a belt of asteroids, chunks of rock and debris ranging in size from dust particles to very small worlds, a few miles on a side. It was once thought that the asteroids represented a planet broken apart by collision, but chemical and isotopic evidence now

[2]For details see *The Third Experiment,* listed in the bibliography at the end of this book.

Jupiter and its moons

indicates that these are instead the remains of the primitive solar system material that never quite made it into a complete planet. Since these asteroids occasionally intersect the orbit of the earth and rain down on us as meteorites, they have given us invaluable clues to the process of solar system formation; much that will be said in this book about the solar system and its origin comes directly from experiments on meteorites.

And now we leave the realm of terrestrial bodies and come into a wholly new and different system of worlds. Jupiter, the largest planet in the solar system, is a totally alien kind of thing. It is composed mostly of elements that on earth are gases—hydrogen and helium—but because of Jupiter's great mass, they are gravitationally compressed into forms of existence we don't see on earth.

The planet is a sort of solar system of its own, with a family of moons circling it just as the planets circle the sun (see photo). Jupiter shows a series of brightly colored parallel bands, which can easily be seen from earth with a good telescope, and the Giant Red Spot. All of these features are due to the planet's being composed of gases. As it rotates, the gases whirl around. The white stripes are expanding gases, rising up high into the atmosphere; when they cool off up there, they spill over into reddish belts and fall back down. The rapid rotation keeps the gaseous stripes and belts lined up parallel to the equator.

The Great Red Spot is an atmospheric disturbance, something like a hurricane, although it is itself bigger than the entire earth and has been there for more than three hundred years, ever since people first looked at Jupiter through a telescope. And this is only the beginning of the strangeness of the planet, compared with earth.

The atmosphere is mostly hydrogen gas, but by the time one sinks through the first 15,000 miles of that atmosphere, the pressure is so intense that the hydrogen has been converted into a metallic state, although it remains a fluid. The temperature at the top of the atmosphere is about -113 degrees centigrade, but inside that dense thicket of gases little heat can escape, and the temperature rises to 30,000 degrees. One way and another, it is not a pleasant place in which to live, and almost certainly nothing does live there—although it has been suggested that the bright colors may indicate some sort of living cells floating around in the atmosphere, somewhere between the too-cold temperatures at the top and the too-hot temperatures at the bottom.

4. Nearly a billion miles from earth lies Saturn, the ringed planet (See photo). With the largest family of moons in the solar system, one of which is just about as big as Mercury, it, too, forms its own planetary system. The rings are not continuous sheets of material, but are formed of small icy particles, perhaps with rocky cores. Saturn is also striped, like Jupiter, but with yellowish to greenish colors instead of red and white, probably due to the crystallization of small molecules at different temperatures between the lighter equator and the darker poles. Due to its great distance, we really knew very little about Saturn until the

Saturn

Voyager spacecraft visited it in 1981, and much of the information gleaned then is still being analyzed.

Even farther away are Uranus and Neptune, and until *Voyager* reached Uranus we knew little about it except that it appeared to be a green-blue blur when viewed from earth. The photo on page 124 shows what it looked like to *Voyager 2* as the spacecraft came whirling over Miranda, one of its moons.

Uranus has a ring system similar to Saturn's but not at all as spectacular. (It now seems that all the Jovian planets have rings.) It and Neptune are composed of some rocky material, some hydrogen and helium, and mostly frozen water, methane, and ammonia. It is probably methane in

123

Uranus

the atmosphere that gives both planets their characteristic color. Neptune, at the present time, is still nothing but a blur to us, although we expect *Viking 2* to reach it in August 1989. Page 125 gives an artist's impression of what it will look like, as seen from the surface of its moon, Triton.

124

An artist's impression of Neptune

Uranus lies on its side, so that its north pole points directly at the sun during the summer and directly away from it during the winter. This is a terribly difficult thing to reconcile with any theory of origin of the planets—as is the backward spin of Venus—and we'll have to be very clever about explaining it.

And finally Pluto. This is the best picture we have of it, which should go a long way toward explaining why we know so little about it. It's nearly four billion miles away, and there isn't much chance of sending a spacecraft there within our lifetimes. Although recent measurements are beginning to reveal some of the planet's mysteries, our knowledge is still too rudimentary for us to include it when considering the origin of the planets, and so we will reluctantly pretend it isn't there.

Now then, let's talk about how to make a typical planet.

Pluto

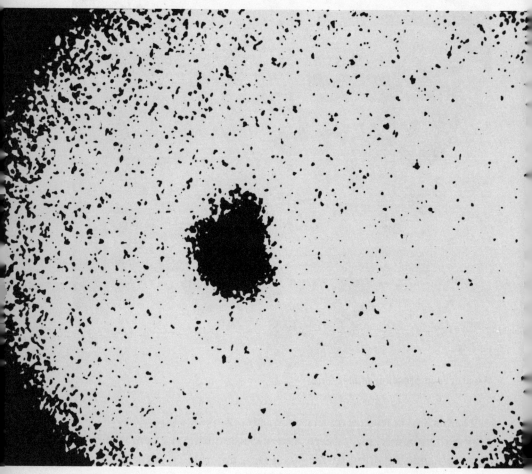

TWENTY-TWO
The Age of the Earth

I. IN THE LATE EIGHTEENTH CENTURY THE FIRST "MODern" geologist, James Hutton, put forth the idea that "the present is the key to the past," that the earth we see today was formed by the same slow and continuous geological processes we see today, working over untold eons of time. In Hutton's day most people still believed Bishop Ussher's seventeenth-century estimate of the age of the earth; Ussher had simply added up all the ages of the patriarchs listed in the Bible, added subsequent recorded history, and finally put in the six days of creation and one day for the Lord to rest and had concluded that the earth was created at 2:30 P.M. on Sunday, October 23, 4004 B.C. Hutton, on the other hand, maintained that much more time was needed to erode the mountains, to wash the sands into smooth shape, and to form all the geological structures we see today. He couldn't estimate the age, but maintained that it was unbelievably large, much larger than a few thousand years. He wrote that he saw in the geological record "no vestige of a beginning, no prospect of an end."

He didn't mean by that statement that he thought the earth had had no beginning, but simply that it was lost in the mists of time. A long time was necessary if the earth had been slowly molded to its present shape, for we do not see such changes taking place within historical time. The Himalayas have "always" been there, the Mississippi has "always" flowed, the Atlantic Ocean has "always" washed our shores.

But not if Hutton was right; there must have been a time when different mountains and different rivers and oceans marked the surface of our planet, and that time must have been long ago compared with the age of man. If Bishop Ussher was right, if the Bible gives an accurate and precise story of the creation, then the time is at least roughly

127

constrained; perhaps setting the date of creation at precisely 9:00 A.M. on a particular day of a particular year is overstating the case a bit, but certainly the earth cannot be more than a few thousand years old.

Since the age of the earth is a crucial point of contention between the Biblical literalists and scientists, and since it is such an interesting example of how science works, and since no history of the earth can be complete without an estimate of when this world was created, let's talk about it.

2. The first realistic estimates of the age of the earth came in the nineteenth century, from two distinctly different sources. The first attack on the biblical point of view came from England's Lord Kelvin, who made two different calculations.

In the first he tried to estimate how the sun provided its energy. Not knowing about nuclear energy, which had not yet been discovered in 1866, he took up an earlier suggestion that the sun was continually attracting by its gravity small interplanetary bodies like meteorites; these, falling into the sun, liberated their gravitational energy and thus kept the sun hot. Knowing the temperature of the sun and the amount of heat it radiates, and estimating the number of such objects floating around the solar system, he calculated that such a process would last for about twenty million years.

Next he assumed that the earth had formed hot and had subsequently cooled off. This seemed reasonable from two points of view: First, the sun was hot and, as we said before, the sun itself constitutes 99 percent of the solar system. Presumably, Kelvin thought, the earth formed in some way from the sun and was therefore hot at the time of its creation. Second, Kelvin happened to be acquainted with a gentleman who owned one of Britain's largest coal mines. It was common knowledge among men conversant with coal mining that as one descended deep into the earth, the temperatures rose.

And remember, the deepest coal mine ever dug barely scratches the surface of the earth. If we think of the earth as an apple, we have not yet burrowed deeper than the skin. So it was quite reasonable to assume that the earth formed hot and cooled from the surface inward, as heat was radiated away from the surface into space, and that today we have a hot internal earth but a cool surface.

Finally, knowing the rate at which rocks can transfer heat (their *thermal conductivity*), he was able to calculate how long it would take a hot earth to cool down to its present temperature. The result was about twenty-five million years.

Taking into account the uncertainties in both calculations, Kelvin rightly felt that the agreement between the two methods was excellent, and justified both assumptions. He wrote that, unless some new source of energy for the sun was thought of and unless someone came up with a better idea of how the earth was formed, his ideas were likely to be true: The sun was heated by meteoric infall, the earth had formed hot, and both were about twenty to twenty-five million years old.

Such an age was long enough to satisfy Hutton's criterion of "no vestige of a beginning" and was quite long enough to incur the wrath of the people who felt the Bible spoke literal truth. But worse was coming.

3. John Joly was an Irish geologist with the temerity to challenge both the physicists and the churchmen. He made a totally different sort of calculation, based on Hutton's philosophy and the eternal question: Why is the ocean salty?

This is a question asked by every intelligent child upon first encountering the ocean and swallowing a mouthful of it. Usually the answers given by one's parents are rather ludicrous. When I was young, I had been told that in ancient days a ship carrying a salt-making machine had sunk, and the machine had never been turned off. A friend of mine was told simply that this was the way God had made the oceans.

Joly, in 1898, used Hutton's suggestion to find the true answer. The oceans are formed by rivers flowing into them. The rivers are formed by lakes draining into them. The lakes are formed by clouds raining into them. The clouds are formed by water evaporating from the oceans.

This is the *hydrologic cycle*: Water evaporates from the oceans and rains back down again. If the clouds drift over land before giving up their rain, the water runs over the land and settles into depressions, forming lakes. Eventually the lakes fill up and spill over their lowest point, forming rivers that run back down to the oceans.

As the rivers run over the earth on their way home again, they dissolve part of the earth. Salts, chemical compounds found in the earth, are reasonably soluble in water; in particular sodium and chloride, which together form the most common salt, called simply *table salt* or even just *salt,* is the most soluble of all. So by the time the rivers travel hundreds and thousands of miles, washing over the earth, they have picked up a small but not insignificant amount of such salts, which are carried along and deposited into the oceans.

Not only are the salts easily soluble in water, but they are extremely difficult to evaporate. You can see this easily in an experiment we discussed earlier: Fill a dish with water and dissolve some salt in it. Let it stand for a day or two, and the water will evaporate, leaving the salt crystals behind.

The same thing happens in the ocean, except that there is too much water for it all to evaporate, and so the salt stays in solution. But as the water continually evaporates into the air, the salt is left behind; as the rivers bring in more water with more salt, the total salt content of the oceans continually increases.

Joly measured how much salt was in the oceans in his day and how much was carried in by rivers; from this he could calculate how long it had taken for the oceans to become as salty as they were. As with Kelvin's method, Joly's method had sources of error: He couldn't measure all the rivers in the world but had to use some average value, and he had to assume that the rate of evaporation and of salt delivery hadn't changed throughout time. Taking these problems into account, he was satisfied that the whole process would take *at least* one hundred million years.

He was satisfied, but neither the physicists nor the bishops were. Kelvin had shown that the sun couldn't be older than 25 million years, and that the earth would be a much colder place than it is if it were older than that, so how could the oceans be at least 100 million years old? And the biblical enthusiasts, of course, stuck to their notion of just a few thousand years.

4. This is an interesting example of a scientific problem, and it shows the power of science to find its way to the truth. Most scientists felt that Kelvin was more likely to be right than Joly, because there were more ways for Joly to be wrong: Temperatures in the past might have been different, which would have affected the rate of evaporation and rainfall, and the rate of river supply to the oceans might have been

different in the past or might be different in different parts of the world even today. For example, people hadn't been able to measure the salt contents of the Amazon and Niger rivers or of those draining much of China and Russia.

In order for Kelvin to be wrong, on the other hand, someone would have to find a new energy source for the sun, and no one could think of one. In addition, someone would have to find an energy source inside the earth to keep it from cooling down as rapidly as Kelvin had calculated.

But such arguments are tentative at best. What was needed was some new experimental data, and until they were forthcoming, most scientists preferred to say that the question of the age of the earth remained open.

The answer came just a few years later, when Henri Becquerel in Paris discovered radioactivity. His work, and particularly that of Marie and Pierre Curie, who followed him, showed that uranium was changing to different elements, and accompanying this process of radioactive decay was the *expenditure of tremendous amounts of energy.*

At first no one could understand where this energy came from, until Einstein in 1905 taught us all that $E = mc^2$, whereupon people found that the decay products of uranium weighed less than the uranium atom itself, and that the difference in mass had been transformed into energy.

This was precisely the new form of energy that Kelvin had missed. Immediately there was a flood of letters to such scientific journals as *Nature* in England, pointing out that this might be the source both of the sun's energy and the earth's slow cooling.[1]

A few years later a young New Zealand scientist, Ernest Rutherford, working in Canada, showed that the earth and the sun were actually *billions* of years old.

5. The technique he used has come to be called *radioactive dating.* To understand it, consider a volcano. Before eruption the molten rock is under the ground. It is composed of many different elements, such as magnesium, aluminum, silicon, oxygen, and potassium. It is potassium that is important to us now, because it is radioactive. One of its isotopes, K-40 (the symbol comes from its Latin name *Kalium*), decays to argon

---

[1]As we discussed earlier, the sun actually uses a different nuclear process, the fusion of hydrogen into helium.

(Ar-40). The half-life is 1.3 billion years, which means that every 1.3 billion years half the potassium-40 atoms decay.[2]

So while the magma is under the ground, some of the potassium is decaying to argon. But argon is a gas (1 percent of the air we breathe is argon), and so when the volcano erupts and the molten magma shoots up into the air, all of the argon bubbles out into the atmosphere.

Then the magma hardens into a rock. And the potassium continues to decay. But any argon produced after solidification will be caught within the crystal structure of the rock and can't bubble out and be lost.

When the rock first forms, a certain amount of potassium is in it and therefore a certain amount of the isotope potassium-40; an average amount would be 0.0001 percent. No argon is in it, because all the argon has been lost upon eruption. One half-life later, half the potassium-40 will have decayed into argon (ignoring the formation of calcium), and so the rock will now contain 0.00005 percent potassium-40 and 0.00005 percent argon-40. The ratio Ar-40/K-40 at the time the rock was created was $0/0.0001 = 0$. One half-life later (1.3 billion years later) the ratio would be $0.00005/0.00005 = 1$. As time increases, the amount of potassium decreases and the amount of argon increases; the ratio is a continually increasing function of the time that has elapsed.

So all you have to do is measure the potassium and argon in a rock, and you can tell how old it is. This is radioactive dating.

And this is what Rutherford did. Actually, of course, many problems have to be worked out for every different kind of rock; many different experimental details have to be checked. Rutherford's first work, in fact, used the decay of uranium to helium instead of potassium to argon, but the principle is the same.

The method doesn't give the age of the earth, but obviously the earth must be *at least* as old as the oldest rock on its surface, and Rutherford found some rocks as old as a billion years. When he presented his results at a lecture in England attended by Lord Kelvin, he pointed out that Kelvin's estimate of the earth's age had been made on the assumption that there was no unthought-of energy source but in fact we now knew

[2]Some of the atoms decay to calcium-40 instead of argon, but this can be corrected for by proper mathematics.

that there was one. Nuclear energy, which gives us the process of radio-active dating, could also provide the energy of the sun and since many atoms of both potassium and uranium are inside the earth, nuclear energy would provide a heat source for the earth, which must have slowed down its rate of cooling.

Other methods of radioactive dating have since been worked out. One in particular, based on the decay of uranium into lead, can integrate data from all over the earth and thus provide an age for the total earth. The answer is 4.6 billion years, with an error estimate of only 0.1 billion years. This fits perfectly with the nuclear energy for the sun; the hydro-gen-helium fusion process should keep the sun on the main sequence for 10 billion years, and so we are confident in saying that the earth and—as indicated by measurements on the moon and meteorites—the rest of the solar system were formed 4.6 billion years ago. This puts the sun about halfway through its lifetime, giving us another 5 billion years or so before it reaches the red-giant stage, when we will have to search for another place to live.

6. None of this has anything to do with the concept of God; none of this argues either for or against the existence of God. To say that the earth was created 4.6 billion years ago instead of a few thousand years ago has nothing to do with whether it was created by a Jewish or Christian or pagan God or by anyone or anything at all. It says only that the Bible cannot be taken as a source of complete and literal truth.

We have by now done many different measurements using several different techniques of radioactive dating on many different kinds of rocks, and we no longer have any "reasonable doubt" that 4.6 billion years is a very good measure of the age of the earth; it is one of the best experimentally determined numbers that we know. The age of the uni-verse is very uncertain, and some day people may say it is twelve or twenty or even 30 billion years old. But don't let anyone tell you that the earth is younger than four and a half or older than 5 billion years. (Of course, if someone does prove me wrong, I'd have to accept it and change my mind. But if anyone wants to bet with you, take the bet. It'll be safer than putting your money in the bank, and you really can't ask for better than that in this shifting, imperfect, and imperfectly under-stood world.)

TWENTY-THREE
Two Theories

I. A FAMILY OF PLANETS LIKE THE ONE WE HAVE circling the sun can be created in two ways. Both were first suggested in simple, rudimentary form within a few years of each other, as if, after thousands of years, people suddenly began to realize the existence of a problem here, that the world we live on had not existed forever but must somehow have come into being.

The first way was suggested by the German philosopher Immanuel Kant, who envisaged a cloud of gas and dust condensing under its own gravity to form the planets. This is similar to our current ideas about star formation, but Kant's theory was more a philosophical than a scientific conjecture, being expressed nonmathematically and thus not open to testing and verification or refutation. But Pierre Laplace, a French mathematician, put it into workable order, whereupon an American scientist, F. R. Moulton, found severe problems with it.

In the Kant-Laplace theory a cloud of gas and dust condensed to form the sun. As it condensed, it left some material behind; it is this left-behind material that in turn condensed to form the individual planets. Moulton's calculations indicated that such material would have spiraled into the sun instead of forming separate planets, and that when it did, it would have made the sun spin much faster than is observed. You see why it is so important to put theories in strict mathematical form. When this is done, they can be made to give mathematical predictions that can then be compared with observations.

Moulton and a colleague, Thomas Crowder Chamberlin, then resurrected a different model to explain the solar system. Just a few years after Kant, the French Comte de Buffon had suggested that a giant comet might have hit the sun and might have caused an explosion that would have shot out solar material, which might then have condensed. Some of the material would have fallen back into the sun, and some would have been lost to space; but some might have fallen into orbit around the sun and thus formed the planets.

In the years following Buffon we learned that his explanation was wrong, for two very good reasons. First, comets turned out to be wispy little things, with not enough mass to cause a solar explosion of the kind demanded. Second, if you'll remember the first chapter of this part of the book, all the planets revolve around the sun in a quite orderly way, all moving in the same direction in the same plane, and nearly all spinning in that same direction. A solar explosion that spouted out material would do so in all directions; the resulting solar system would look quite chaotic, with planets moving and spinning in all directions and in all planes.

Moulton and Chamberlin suggested that instead of a comet, a wandering star might remove the first objection; the second objection was met by modifying the theory so that the wandering star didn't actually collide with the sun but passed close by. As it passed by, its gravity pulled out the surface material of the sun, just as the black hole in Cyg X-1 pulls out its partner's material, and as the star passed on and disappeared, some of the ejected material fell back onto the sun and some of it fell into orbit *around* the sun, thence to form the planets.

But within the past few decades the mathematical objections to the condensation theory (which had been pointed out by Moulton) have been eliminated. Hannes Alfven, a Swedish electrical engineer, pointed out that the sun's magnetic field, which had been unknown in Moulton's time, would have pushed out against the left-behind material of the condensation and would have acted as a brake to keep it from falling into the sun. Other scientists in Europe, the Soviet Union, and the United States followed up by showing that the condensation theory is in excellent agreement with our ideas on star formation. As a cloud of gas and dust condenses to form a star, igniting its hydrogen-helium furnace at the center, it would be very likely to gather about it a halo of material that would spin down into a disk around the forming star's equator. As the material in the disk bounced around, the particles would attract each other, either by mutual gravity or magnetic effects or by other mechanisms still being argued about, and such a situation would in fact be very likely to end by providing the planets we see today. It is now the general consensus that this is probably the correct explanation for the origin of the planets.

Meanwhile work on the near-collision theory has also continued, and its mathematics have been worked out in great detail, primarily by Dr. M. M. Woolfson of York University in England. Though most scientists feel strongly that such an unlikely event as this theory depends upon is unlikely to have produced our solar system, "feelings" do not constitute proof.

So then. How are we going to be able to prove which of the two theories is the correct one?

Why, by testing them, of course. By observation.

But what should we observe in order to test them? We can't go back in time to actually see what happened, can we?

Can't we?

TWENTY-FOUR
To Test a Theory

I. WHEN YOU WANT TO TEST A THEORY, YOU ASK what it predicts and then you look for it. But you have to be particular about what you're asking it to predict. If I have a theory that my sister is a two-headed creep, I must ask what the theory predicts. That is, what does a two-headed creep look like? Well, it's sort of creepy, and it has two heads and probably two arms and two legs. When I look at my sister, I do indeed observe that she has two arms and two legs. Does that prove she's a two-headed creep?

She might indeed be one, but the theory has hardly been proved because of that prediction. You have to ask the theory what it predicts *that other theories don't.* In particular, when you're trying to decide between two theories, you have to ask what each of them predicts that is different from what the other predicts and then look to see which one is right.

The condensation theory of planet formation is based on the general inefficiency of the universe. When some people look out at the universe, they see it working like a perfectly tuned clock, with every piece in the proper position, ticking away perfectly for eternity. Those people are not looking very closely.

Life, for example, which is an intrinsic part of the universe, is notoriously wasteful. Oak trees produce scores and scores of acorns for each one that eventually becomes a new tree, and this same procedure is followed by virtually every life form. Female humans produce an egg every month for thirty or forty years, and on an average only two or three of these four hundred eggs are ever used. And if you think about the number of sperm that one male produces in his lifetime, with all but two or three being wasted—!

Other aspects of the universe are just as inefficient. The purest crystal ever formed will have billions of atomic impurities in it. More water rains over the oceans than over the lands, accomplishing nothing. Some of the chemical elements that formed in stars are the result of processes that give the stars their energy, but most of the elements are formed by the neutron capture processes, which provide no energy at all, which are simply a wasteful side process, occurring only because of the inefficiency of the whole setup.

The condensation theory says that when stars form by condensation of a hydrogen cloud, that process, too, will be inefficient. Not all the material of the cloud will be sucked into the forming star; some of it will be left behind. As far as the star is concerned, this material is simply wasted.

Furthermore, the star will be spinning. This is because the cloud, as it begins to contract, must have some angular momentum acquired as it went tumbling through the galaxy. Conservation of angular momentum insists that as the cloud contracts, it must spin more and more rapidly (as discussed on page 98). This spinning motion will slide the left-behind material into a disk around the central star. This is because only two forces are acting at this time: gravity, which is directed equally in all directions, and centrifugal force, which is directed outward in the plane of the spinning equator. The result will be an overall force into the plane of the equator.

So the star reaches a stage where it consists of a central bulge of material, in the interior of which nuclear reactions begin to take place, and a disk whirling around it.

As more and more material slides down into the disk, small particles of dust will begin to come together at random. If they are iron and thus magnetic, or if they are carbon and thus able to join with many other elements, or merely if they bump together gently enough, their mutual gravity will begin to hold them together. Once that happens, the new, bigger particle will have stronger gravity and will be able to absorb other particles. In time large bodies begin to grow, sweeping up all other material in their path. Computer simulations of the process indicate that in this way the terrestrial planets may grow.

The disk is composed of the same material as the sun, mostly hydrogen and helium. These gases do not form dust particles, but in the disk are some heavier elements formed in previous stars; it is this material that becomes the terrestrial planets. The hydrogen and helium, being light and gaseous, are mostly lost to space or pulled into the sun.

Farther out in the disk, far away from the developing central star, the temperatures are much lower. The abundant molecules of water may freeze out there, and so planets forming there may incorporate much more water into their mass than do terrestrial planets, which form closer to the sun. This makes the outer planets large enough to attract and hold hydrogen and helium gravitationally in addition to water and the heavier elements. Since there is so much more hydrogen and helium than anything else, the planets will grow to much larger sizes than the warmer, interior planets that have lost these gases. The outer planets will be so big, in fact, that as they form they leave behind their own planetary disks, which go through the same process again, though on a smaller scale. Part of the disk remains as a system of rings around the planet; the rest forms moons.

Though this has been told in skimpy detail, the major provisions of planetary formation are there. While we have skipped the question of differences among the major planets, the plan does explain why the Jovian planets, farther from the sun, are bigger; why they are composed mostly of light elements while the terrestrial planets contain mostly heavier elements; why they have moons while the terrestrial planets do not; and why their densities are lower. (The plan does not explain the spins of Venus, Uranus, and Pluto or the mass and motion of Pluto or the existence of the moons of earth and Mars. A recent speculation involves a few catastrophic collisions of the planets with nearly planet-sized objects toward the end of the formation process. Such a collision with earth might have splashed out the material that formed our moon, while similar collisions but with slightly different parameters might have reversed Venus's spin and knocked Uranus and Pluto on their sides. This wraps up most of what we know fairly neatly, if we assume that the Martian moons are merely captured asteroids. But it's all very iffy, so there is still lots of work to be done, lots of fun to be had.)

Now what about the wandering star theory? How is it different?

2. The wandering star hypothesis starts from another viewpoint entirely. First, it rejects the notion that the left-behind material from star formation will necessarily form a disk that will self-aggregate into planets. The material might just as well spin off into space and be lost.

Instead, this scenario concentrates on the mechanics of the motion of stars in our galaxy. The Milky Way galaxy is a typical sort of galaxy, spiral in shape with a concentration of stars at its center that spills over into rotating spiral arms. Our own sun is roughly two-thirds of the way out along one of those spiral arms and rotates around the galactic center once every two hundred million years. This rotational motion is determined, like all astronomical motions in the universe, by gravity. Just as, in the solar system, the inner planets circle the sun in a shorter time than do the outer ones, so in the galaxy do the inner stars. This means there is a relative motion among the galaxy's stars: As our sun, for example, rotates around the center, it comes up and passes those farther away and is in turn passed by those closer in.

New stars are also forming throughout the galaxy, throughout time, and all this together means that stars are continually passing by one another. We see experimental proof of this when we look at the Doppler shifts of other stars in our galaxy. Some are redshifted, some are blue, which means that some stars are receding from us while other stars are approaching. Eventually, then, some stars must collide.

We have already seen that a stellar collision will not give rise to a planetary system like ours, since the planets that might be born in such a collision would not all orbit in a single plane. But if occasionally stars may collide, then also they may have near-misses, and that is what the wandering-star hypothesis concentrates on.

A star wanders by the sun, pulls material out of it, and some of this material falls into orbit around the sun and congregates into planets. Alternatively, it might be the sun that pulls material from the passing star, and it is that material that then falls into orbit around the sun.

Once this occurs, the model is similar to the first one. The material will aggregate by collisions, which lead to gravitational attraction, and slowly the planets will build themselves out of this material. As in the first theory, material closer to the sun will be warm, and thus no hydrogen or helium will condense into these inner planets; the outer material will be colder and will allow such hydrogen and helium aggregation. The nature of the planets will be much the same in either theory.

How, then, can we decide between the two models?

3. There is one basic difference between them. The condensation model says that planetary formation is a normal part of star formation; therefore large numbers of stars should have planets. The wandering star theory, on the other hand, says that planets form only when one star encounters another. How frequently would this happen?

First of all, we have to note that more is required than simply that one star should come somewhere near another. We have to ask *how near?* If they approach too closely, their mutual gravitational attraction will pull them into each other, and we have already seen that such a collision would not result in our planetary system. If they pass too far from each other, not enough material would be pulled out and it would not fall back into proper orbits.

It turns out, when one goes through the complex mathematics, that the approach must take place within very rigid boundaries, depending on the masses of the stars and their relative velocities as well as the distance of closest approach. Taking into account all the stars in the galaxies and what we know of average distances between them and relative motions within the overall galactic motion, we can calculate that such a process might result in a solar system like ours perhaps once every 10 billion years.

Since the galaxy is roughly 10 billion years old, that means it might have happened once.

But such a statistical analysis is extremely imprecise when it points to a single event. The result actually means that it might have happened once, or zero times, or perhaps twice, or even three times. The important point is that it is not a *usual* event in the galaxy.

And so here we have our point of departure between the two theories. The wandering-star theory says that of the hundred billion stars in the galaxy, at most another one or two planetary systems might be similar to our own. The condensation theory says that such planetary systems should form rather generally, and so billions of planetary systems should be in the galaxy.

4. Some people have used this argument to deny the validity of the wandering-star theory. They say that if you have two possibilities, one of which is normal and usual, while the other depends on a highly unlikely event, then obviously the more normal, likely event is more likely to have happened.

But this ignores a great ignorance of ours. We do not know if our solar system is a usual sort of thing or not. If, in fact, no other star in the galaxy has a planetary system like ours, then it follows that our solar system was created in some sort of highly unusual event. It is only if we find planets like ours duplicated around many other stars that we can argue that the system of planetary formation must be a normal, usual sort of thing.

So the observation we have to make is obvious: We have to look at other stars and see if they have planetary systems like ours. Are we alone in this universe or not?

TWENTY-FIVE
Other Worlds

I. THE QUESTION SEEMS SIMPLE, BUT THE ANSWER AT present is nearly totally unknown.

Suppose you were living somewhere else in the universe and wanted to determine if there were planets around our sun. The simplest thing would be to come here and take a look, but Einstein and the vastness of the universe say that you can't.

Remember Einstein's formula for the mass of a moving object? He said that the mass m is related to the mass of the object at rest m_o by

$$m = m_o/\sqrt{(1 - v^2/c^2)}.$$

So what happens when you or your spaceship or anything at all goes as fast as light? That would mean that your velocity v is equal to c, so that the mass

$$m = m_o/\sqrt{(1 - c^2/c^2)}$$

$$= m_o/\sqrt{(1 - 1)}$$

$$= m_o/0$$

And this means that the mass moving at the velocity of light is equal to infinity, since any number divided by zero is infinite. Since $E = mc^2$, it would take an infinite amount of energy to make an infinite mass. No motor or propulsion system could possibly provide an infinite amount of energy, so we arrive at a rigid conclusion of Einstein's equations: Nothing with any original mass can travel as fast as light.[1]

[1]Since photons have zero rest mass (m_o), they are not affected by this consideration.

This will inevitably limit our exploration of the universe. No matter how clever we are, or how much energy we are willing to consume in our spaceship, if Einstein's theory is correct, we can never reach the speed of light.

This is, of course, an unimportant restriction on our travels around the earth and even within the solar system. To reach Mars at the speed of light, for example, would take 19 minutes. So even going half that fast, it would take only a bit more than half an hour. (In actual fact, at the present time we can't go anywhere near such speeds.)

But to travel to other stars is a different matter. The closest stars to us are Alpha Centauri and Barnard's Star, and these are several light-years away. (Distances to the stars are so vast that we measure them in light-years instead of in miles. One light-year is the distance light travels in one year; at a speed of 186,000 miles per second that comes to 5.87×10^{12} miles.) So at the highest speed imaginable, ignoring any technical difficulties, it would still take several years to get to these stars and then several years to come home again.

And these are the *nearest* stars. Only a very few stars are within a dozen light-years; most are hundreds and thousands and hundreds of thousands of light-years away, which makes it absolutely impossible to visit them. (To give just one argument in this line: What president is going to plead for taxes to provide funds for such a spaceship when no result of the trip can be known for a hundred thousand years—and the government goes out of office in four years?)

2. So how can we tell if these other stars have planets? The only thing to do is to look at them, but here again we run into problems.

Planets shine by the reflected light of their star, and they shine extremely dimly by comparison. Venus, for example, is much closer to us than is the sun, but the sun is incomparably brighter. Mercury is also closer to us than is the sun, and we can barely see it because it is hidden in the sun's glare.

We have the same problem—magnified by the tremendous distances involved—when we look for planets around other stars. A planet the size of the earth would simply not reflect enough light to keep from being hidden in the glare of its parent star. We have to adopt more subtle methods.

One is to look back in time. We ended a previous chapter by asking if that were possible. It is, in the sense that we can look at stars younger than our sun and see them as they develop—as our sun developed four and a half billion years ago. When our solar system was forming, if the condensation theory is correct, it started out as a disk of gas and dust surrounding the central star. So two scientists, Bradford Smith and Richard Terrile, decided to look for such disks around young stars.

They still had the problem that the disk would not be as bright as the star and would be hidden in its glare. So they used a technique originally designed to look at our sun's outer gases by shielding the central mass. And they were able to obtain a photo that shows a disk of material around the young star Beta Pictoris. It may be what our solar system looked like when it was just beginning to form.

Two other scientists, Donald McCarthy and Frank Low, used a different technique. Since most stars emit most light in the visible region, while planets absorb this and reemit a lot of light in the infrared wavelength region, they decided to look for planets in the infrared. In 1984 they succeeded in finding what looked like a definite planet around the star van Biesbroeck 8.

Both these experiments were exciting but not conclusive. The disk around Beta Pictoris may be the beginning of a planetary system, but maybe it's something different we don't understand yet. And the planet around van Biesbroeck 8 presents two problems. The first and most important problem is that the planet has disappeared. No one has been able to see it in the several years since its discovery, and the general suspicion today is that the original data were somehow mistaken.

The second problem is that, even if the planet does exist, it's several dozen times bigger than Jupiter, which makes it as big as the smallest stars. So the system would be closer to a binary star than to a planetary system.

What we really want to know is whether planets similar to earth can form as a natural consequence of star formation, whether they exist in profusion throughout the galaxy. And we still don't know. Planets as small as the earth are just too hard to see.

A promising method is to look for the effect of the planet's gravitational attraction on the star. If the star has planets around it, they will tug on it; the result will be that the star, instead of moving in a smooth curve on its journey through the galaxy, will wobble. In 1937 Peter van de Kamp thought he had detected such a wobble in the motion of Barnard's Star, but it has since been disproved or, at least (like van Biesbroeck 8), thrown into doubt.

However, in 1987 a Canadian group of astronomers, using a new technique to look for this effect, announced that they had found planets around two of sixteen nearby stars. But again these planets are larger than Jupiter and so are nothing like earth or the sun's family of planets. So we still haven't seen anything resembling our own solar system.

And we probably won't for a long time yet. Plans have been made for flying satellites and space telescopes with precision much improved over our earth-based systems, but even these won't be quite good enough to find what we hope is out there. By a combination of the techniques discussed above, they should be able to detect major-sized planets around the nearest stars. But we don't have anything even in the construction stage that will be able to see earth-sized planets, and so we still have quite a few years of speculation ahead of us.

TWENTY-SIX
Hello Out There!

I. THERE'S ONE OTHER WAY TO FIND OUT IF ANY OTHER planets exist, and that's to sit back and listen. The idea is to direct sensitive radio receivers out into space and listen for someone signaling to us.

The chain of reasoning is that if other planets exist, some of them should be suitable for life; if planets suitable for life exist, life will evolve on them; if they have existed as long as earth, life will have reached an intelligent, technological level; if intelligent creatures exist, they will attempt to contact others throughout the galaxy; and if they do, radio transmission is the most intelligent way to do this.

Let's get that last assumption out of the way first, since it has the least arguments against it (although, as we'll see later, it's possible to argue against anything if you set your mind to it). We have seen that the velocity of light is a limit to the ease of star travel, and when you combine that with the sheer size of the galaxy, the task of exploring it takes on whole new dimensions.

On earth we began to explore as soon as we were able, and that statement applies to human beings all over the globe. In the Pacific, natives of the islands set out in sailing canoes over the seemingly infinite wastes of the waters to see what was beyond the horizon. They found and colonized islands thousands of miles from their native shores. In Asia the ancient Chinese crossed the seas and colonized Japan, while Indians spread out in both directions from their early cities. The civilization that began in the Tigris-Euphrates valley moved out into Africa and Europe, and of course we are familiar since school days with the great circumpolar navigations of the European peoples and with their discovery of our own land. We, in our turn, have gone to the moon and sent spaceships to Venus and Mars.

But the earth and even the solar system are tiny places compared with the galaxy. The galaxy consists of a hundred billion stars, and even if we limit the number of interesting ones to those no bigger than the sun—since larger ones will evolve and die too quickly to allow intelligent life to develop on whatever planets they might have—that still leaves a staggering number. And when you add to this the difficulty caused by the distances between stars, which averages more than a thousand light-years each, you can see the impossibility of setting up human-operated spaceships to go visiting to see what's out there.

The same problems apply, of course, to nonhuman-operated space-ships, and that is why the stories of flying saucers zooming down on lonely rural highways to frighten people on their way home are non-sense. Unless we are wrong about relativity, unless some way of beating the speed limit exists—something like time-warps or dimensionality-transfers, science-fiction stuff—the relativistic speed limit will stop any physical exploration of the galaxy by anyone, anywhere.[1]

Radio exploration has its own very real limitations, but it has unques-tionable advantages over spaceships. First of all, radio waves do travel at the speed of light, which is the fastest anything can go. Second, and more important, you can beam a radio wave out in all directions at the same time. You don't have to send a beam out to just one star and then wait for an answer—or the lack of one—before you send another beam out to another star. You can sit on your planet and send out signals continuously to the whole galaxy, or you can pick out a few hundred nearby stars and beam high intensity signals to them.

And then you sit and you wait. There's no avoiding that. Even with radio signals, it will take hundreds and thousands of years for your signal to reach anyone sitting on a planet moving around a typical star and an equal time before their return signal can get back to you. So the explora-tion of the galaxy is going to take a long, long time. (The rest of the universe is even farther away. Distances to other galaxies range from hundreds of thousands of light-years all the way up to billions of light-years. So forget about them.)

[1]Of course the fact that we know of no way to warp space or time in such a magic manner doesn't mean that future generations may not discover how to do it. But the whole point of this book is that we have to stick with what we have evidence for; otherwise, we may as well believe in astrology and creationism and ghosts and hobgoblins and tooth-fairies.

That is why, at our stage of development, we have no choice but to begin by listening rather than transmitting. If we transmit, we won't get a reply within our lifetime; but if there is someone out there already transmitting, all we have to do is tune in.

So what is the chance that someone actually is out there, calling to us?

2. Pretty good. Or at least that's what a lot of people think.

The argument begins, first of all, with the original question of the existence of other planets. If planetary systems are formed only by unusual occurrences, such as near-collisions between wandering stars, then there will be only one or two such systems in the entire galaxy and the chance of intelligent life arising more than once—and reaching out to contact the other across the vast galactic distances—is really remote, not worth thinking about.

But if planets arise as a natural consequence of star formation, then there must be very many of them. If only one percent of stars form planets, then there still are a billion planetary systems in the galaxy.

If that is so, on how many of them will there be at least one planet suitable for life? That means, as far as we know, an earthlike planet[2] with a stable orbit neither too close nor too far from its sun, so that its temperature will remain above the freezing point and below the boiling point of water.

Why is water so important? Because life consists of a series of chemical reactions, which must occur virtually continuously and uninterruptedly. Water provides the perfect medium for such reactions. Because of its peculiar structure, water is the closest thing to a universal solvent we have. Once dissolved, the chemical compounds can move around easily, come into contact with each other, and undergo the complex chemical reactions that lead to and sustain life. Without this process, life becomes terribly unlikely. Solvents other than water may be possible, but water is clearly the best. Water is also formed of two abundant types of atom, hydrogen and oxygen, and can exist as a liquid under a wider range of conditions than most possible substitutes. All in all, water is both the

[2]Perhaps nonearthlike planets might have nonearthlike life? Perhaps. But communicating with creatures at least vaguely earthlike is going to be hard enough, to begin with.

most likely and the best possible solvent for life processes.

Next, the planets we're looking for must have the basic chemicals for life, which means having carbon, hydrogen, and oxygen, at least. We have already seen that these are among the most abundant elements in the universe, hydrogen being the original stuff of the universe and carbon and oxygen being formed as part of the fuel cycle in red giants. So they should exist in abundance on most second-generation stars and on their planets. But—

Is the mere presence of these elements sufficient for the creation of life?

3. One hundred and fifty years ago, people would have said no. They would have said that in order for life to exist, there must be present a magical ingredient that some called the life force and others called the breath of God. But in 1828, in one of the most important scientific experiments of all time, a German scientist named Friedrich Wöhler heated up in a flask a mixture of ammonium cyanate and water and found that he had turned it into the chemical compound *urea,* the basic constituent of urine.

The importance of this experiment is that urea is a chemical produced by the living body. Until this experiment, it had been thought that the chemicals of life were different from the chemicals of nonlife. It was known that *biogenic* chemicals, as they are called, all involve hydrocarbons, compounds of carbon and hydrogen and, usually, oxygen, and that they were not and could not be produced by any nonliving process.

Wöhler changed all that when he created urea in his laboratory. For the first time a biogenic chemical had been created without the magic of a life force, without the breath of a god. Wöhler founded the science of organic chemistry, which is the study of all carbon-based chemistry, and since then we have found no distinction between these compounds, whether they are created in living systems or in the laboratory. In 1954, in fact, Harold Urey and Stanley Miller at the University of Chicago mixed together in a flask some water, ammonia, and carbon dioxide— simple chemicals that would be present on any primitive earthlike planet—and when they passed an electrical discharge through the flask they found that amino acids were produced.

Amino acids are the complex organic chemicals that are the basis of life. This experiment showed that the basic processes on the road to life could be formed by natural processes if the conditions are right.

The right conditions are, first, the presence of water and the proper chemical elements, and second, a source of energy.

On a first-generation star the only elements present will be hydrogen and helium, so no life is present. But after the first few billion stars have gone through their cycles, have synthesized heavier elements in their interiors, and then burst into supernovae and scattered those elements throughout the galaxy, the second generation of stars will form with those elements present, and any planets forming around those stars will also have those elements. Since the elements necessary for life—carbon and oxygen in addition to hydrogen—are among the most abundant elements formed in stellar interiors, we have no problem here.

In the early years of planetary formation, there will be many sources of energy—as indeed there still are today on the earth. There is starlight, or sunlight, of course. And there is lightning and meteoritic impacts and volcanic eruptions. There is no shortage of energy supplies.

We have not yet demonstrated in the laboratory that life will form under these conditions, but our failure to do so is not surprising. Our knowledge of the life processes is still rudimentary, and in fact the formation of the first living cell was not an easy thing on earth: It took nearly one billion years before any evidence of life was preserved in the geologic record. It very likely took close to that time, or at least hundreds of millions of years, for the first life to form. So it's not going to be easy to duplicate that creation in our laboratory, and until we do we can't be sure. It might yet be necessary for some god to breathe the breath of life into a bit of clay to make it live, but I don't think so.

If we accept the proposition that life will form, given the proper chemicals and the proper conditions, then what about the formation of *intelligent* life, which of course is necessary for it to begin sending radio signals out to the galaxy?

4. As far as we know, it's only a question of time. We have to admit that as we come closer and closer to this question of intelligent life, we know less and less. But here on earth we see clearly that life has progressively evolved into more and more complex systems; there certainly is no question about that. The evidence for evolution is clear-cut and

incontrovertible; we see it in the fossil record, in comparative biochemistry and anatomy, and in embryonic developments.

Evolution has progressed so naturally that we take it for granted that it will function wherever life originates, that given enough time any beginning life will evolve into complex forms. As far as we can tell, intelligence is a natural product of such evolution, but here again we have to pause and admit our ignorance. We don't understand intelligence or consciousness, so how can we be sure?

Well, we're not sure. By this stage we are talking about what we think probable, not what we have proved scientifically. The chain of reasoning becomes weaker at each link. Star formation is certainly a continuing process throughout time and space in this universe. Probably planet formation is a natural process accompanying star formation. If so, a certain number of planets will have carbon and oxygen and orbits suitable for liquid water. Life will then probably begin on at least some of these planets. Given enough time (a few billion years), that life should—at least sometimes—evolve intelligence, and intelligence should invent technology and should include curiosity about other possible life forms in the universe and so should send out radio signals to us.

Hidden in this chain of reasoning is the supposition that at least one life form more highly evolved than we are exists—for after all we have not yet evolved to the position of sending out radio signals to the rest of the galaxy.

How likely is such a supposition?

5. Quite likely, indeed. Our star is a fairly typical small star; there are many others like it in the galaxy. It is about four and a half billion years old, and the galaxy is about ten billion years old. Therefore, there are many stars like our sun, both older and younger. In particular, there will be stars in the galaxy many billions of years older than our sun.

Although life on earth began within the first billion years, human life has arisen only within the last few million years. That is, the earth is about 4,600 million years old and was about 4,595 million years old before the first humans appeared. And our technological civilization is only about a hundred years old.

We might expect, then, that a similar star a billion years older could have a civilization a billion years older than we are. Now just consider how advanced our civilization is today over what it was a hundred years ago. At that time there were no airplanes, no rockets, no lasers or television sets, not the slightest hint that such a thing as nuclear energy might exist.

Think what we were like five to ten thousand years ago. We believed in good and wicked gods traveling about the heavens in flaming chariots, we huddled fearfully in caves when the lightning struck, we shivered in terror when the sun went down. Go back a hundred thousand years or so, and you find nothing but naked savages scrounging for berries and running from tigers.

Can you encompass how far we have come in a few thousand years? Now try to consider a tenth of a billion years, a hundred million years? Dinosaurs ruled the earth; there wasn't the faintest trace of humanity.

Can you imagine, if we have come this far in that time, how far we shall have advanced in another hundred million years?

That is how far, presumably, another alien civilization might be if it is a hundred million years older than we are.

And there are stars out there that are *billions* of years older than ours.

6. So, if this chain of reasoning is correct, several billion planetary systems ought to be out there, with perhaps hundreds of millions of them reasonably similar to our own. Tens of millions of planets should be suitable for life, and perhaps millions or at least hundreds of thousands of them on which life actually has developed. On thousands of them life may have reached the level of intelligence, and on hundreds of these there should be technological civilizations more advanced than our own.

And here we sit, wondering if all this is true.

Right at this moment the most exciting experiment in the history of the world is taking place. Scientists are actually listening for alien radio signals in a series of experiments called SETI: the Search for Extraterrestrial Intelligence. Congress in 1983 funded the program at one and a half million dollars a year for five years. The Russians are also actively pursuing a search; in fact, it is probably due to the Russians' activity that Congress finally—after many years of arguing and cajoling by the scientists—was convinced to fund the program.

153

Of course, we may be on the wrong track technologically. A couple of hundred years ago we didn't know that radio waves existed. Perhaps civilizations a few thousand or a few million years more advanced than we are have discovered a better way of communication than radio waves: perhaps we are listening with an outmoded technology for signals that don't exist, while the rest of the galaxy is communicating by a means of which we know nothing. When, for example, the first European radio operators were transmitting around the world in the early decades of this century, natives on the Pacific islands never for a moment suspected that the air around their heads was singing with radio signals on their way to Australia and India.

Perhaps today such unsuspected signals are passing us by, while we sit here deaf and silent, wondering at the universal silence.

Sad, isn't it?

Or, perhaps, wonderful . . . ?

PART IV

PAST AND FUTURE WORLDS
(Dust thou wert, to dust returneth....)

TWENTY-SEVEN

The Cinderella Universe

1. CLEARLY, THE UNIVERSE IS EXPANDING. WE SEE THIS from our observations of the redshifts of the galaxies, and this basic fact was the starting point for our understanding of the past history—indeed the beginning—of the universe. But what does it mean for the future?

If no force operates to restrain this expansion, it must continue forever. But we know that a restraining force exists: Gravity, the attractive force between every two objects in the universe, will try to pull the universe together again. And so we have the universal expansion blowing the universe apart, and gravity trying to pull it together again.

We can think of the universe as a stretching rubber band. The force stretching it is the initial force of the Big Bang, and the elastic force pulling it back together again is the force of gravity. What will happen to such a stretching band?

Clearly, if the stretching force is greater than the restraining force, the band will break and fly apart. But if the restraining force is greater, the expansion will slow and stop, and the band will snap back together again.

Which course will the universe take?

We don't know.

2. It all depends on how much mass there is in the universe. (Strictly speaking, it depends on the mass density of the universe. This can be thought of as the amount of mass in some average volume of space.) If the amount of mass in this average volume is below a critical value, it will not generate enough gravitational force to defeat the expansion; if it is above this critical value, it will.

This can be phrased in general relativistic terms if we talk about the

157

curvature of the universe. You will remember that Einstein said that gravity is really a curvature of space-time, and it turns out that there are three possible types of curvature: positive, negative, and zero (or flat). You will also remember that we said that it is impossible for our human brains to visualize curved three-dimensional spaces (let alone a curved four-dimensional space-time), so once again we have to talk in two-dimensional analogies.

Imagine the curved surface of the earth. This is an example of *positive* curvature. Its main feature, so far as we are concerned, is that it is *closed,* or *finite.* If we restrict ourselves to stay within this two-dimensional space (the surface of the earth)—so that we cannot go shooting off into space or down into the center of the sphere—what happens if we set off on a voyage and never change direction? Imagine that we set sail from Spain, heading west. If we are Columbus, we hit the American continent (or its outlying islands), but imagine that we continue on. Obviously, we will not forever continue to encounter new lands. Eventually we arrive back where we started. *Without ever changing direction.*

This is the basic characteristic of a positively curved space: Motion in any direction in what appears to be a straight line, without change of direction, eventually brings you back to the starting point.

In a positively curved three- or four-dimensional space the same thing would happen. (Physicists talk about the three-dimensional hypersurface of a hypersphere embedded in a four-dimensional space, but you don't have to worry about such things until you get to graduate school.) You would take off from earth in a straight line, never changing direction, and eventually your spaceship would return to earth. (Of course, "eventually" in this case would mean many billions of years later even if you traveled at nearly the speed of light.)

The two-dimensional example of a *negatively* curved space is an ordinary horse's saddle. Imagine that you start at some point on the saddle, and you move upward. What happens? You go up toward the hump, and then you cross over it, and then you head downward *on the other side.* You never come back to where you started from. This is the basic characteristic of a negatively curved, or *open,* space.

It boggles the imagination to try to think of a negatively curved three- or four-dimensional space, but mathematically the equations give the same result: A traveler setting off in a straight-line voyage would continue on forever, and if he never turned around, he would never come home again.

The third possible type of curvature is a precise balance between positive and negative, called zero curvature, corresponding to a perfectly flat space. This would also be infinite in extent.

A positively curved universe would correspond to the situation where gravity overpowers the expansion. The galaxies, which are now flying away from each other, would, in our two-dimensional analogy, go flying around the "sphere" of the universe and all meet up again on the other side. On this side of the sphere (in the past, the present, and the next few eons of the future) they are flying away from each other; on the other side of the sphere (in the far-distant future) they would come flying together again.

A negatively curved universe would correspond to the situation where there is not enough mass to overpower the expansion. The galaxies that are now flying apart would continue forever to recede from each other, disappearing over the "hump" of the "saddle" into the black vastnesses of an infinite space.

In a perfectly flat universe the expansion rate would neither continue forever nor reverse but would go asymptotically[1] to zero.

So what is it going to be? Positive, negative, or zero?

It all depends on the total mass density in the universe. In a simple but complex calculation (that is, simple if you know what you're doing, but too complex to derive here) it turns out that the mass density needed to close the universe[2] is about 10^{-29} grams per cubic centimeter, which is an incredibly small amount. It corresponds to just a few hydrogen atoms in every cubic meter—much better than the best vacuum we can produce on earth. But of course that is averaged throughout the entire universe, much of which is empty interstellar and intergalactic space.

The question then is, What is the actual mass density of the universe? And the problem is that we simply don't know. There is the distinct possibility, in fact, that most of the mass of the universe is invisible.

[1]That is, the rate of expansion would get slower and slower, but the universe would continue to expand. In an infinite time, the expansion would finally stop, but nothing can ever reach infinity.
[2]Closing the universe amounts to having enough gravity to overcome the expansion and begin the reversal or provide a positive curvature.

3. The simplest test would be to look out at the night sky and count up all the mass that we see: stars and clouds of dust and nebulae and whatever. We have done this, and the result turns out to be that the universe has roughly a tenth to a half of the critical density. This would mean that there is not enough mass to close the universe, and so we will expand forever.

But.

But it's so *close.* The density of mass could be any number, from infinitely less than to infinitely greater than the critical number. Then why, a lot of people have been asking, does it just happen to be so close to that critical number?

Coincidence? Of course, that's possible. Coincidences do occur. But one tends to distrust them, especially when the odds against a particular one are so high. If the first person you meet when you walk out of your house in the morning is a man, that's not surprising: The odds were fifty-fifty that it would be. But if the first person you meet is the particular man that you owed money to when you skipped town on the other side of the country fifteen years ago, well, it could be just coincidence, but you'd have to think he probably tracked you down and was waiting for you.

So the coincidence of the measured density being so close to the critical density makes one think that perhaps the true value is *precisely* the critical density. But we don't *see* that much mass.

The suggestion has been made that perhaps this mass exists but is invisible. This idea is not as surprising as it first sounds. We have already encountered invisible mass in one form, the black holes. If enough black holes exist, they could exert enough gravity to close the universe. Research on these objects is just beginning; at the present time they can be observed only if they happen to be part of a binary star system, where we can see their effect on their partner star. If black holes exist remote from any other object, they'd be truly invisible to us. We just wouldn't know if they were there or not.

And there are other possibilities, ranging from the normal to the exotic. A normal example is the possibility of masses of intergalactic dust that could exist hidden in the dark, empty vastnesses of space, unseen and unsuspected. A more exotic possibility is that of neutrino mass.

160

Neutrinos are tiny particles emitted in radioactive decay, and they are known to flood the universe. They are produced, for example, in the nuclear processes that fuel the sun, to such an extent that in any given second, hundreds of thousands of them come flying out of the sun and pass through your body. It is not known if they have any mass. They might be totally massless, in which case they would travel at the speed of light and would not affect the mass density of the universe. But they might have a very tiny mass, and if they do, their total mass would be sufficient to close the universe.

In 1987 a supernova was seen, and neutrinos from it were detected. In principle, comparing the time of arrival of the neutrinos at earth with the time the supernova was first seen—which corresponds to the time of arrival of its light on earth—would tell us the relative velocity of the neutrinos and the light. If the neutrinos travel at the speed of light, they must be massless, since relativity tells us that only massless particles can travel with that velocity. If they have a velocity slower than light, they must have mass. As I write, their possible mass, according to this observation, is very small but not quite zero; the question of whether they might close the universe is not yet answered.

And there are other possibilities, even wilder. Consider cosmic strings, for instance. These are not the tiny superstrings we discussed earlier, but rather gigantic filaments stretching across the universe. The idea is that when the original symmetry broke and the universe was inflated into different domains, sometime within the first 10^{-35} seconds of existence, frozen bits of the original field were trapped into strings with a thickness not much greater than that of a single atom, but with a mass of about ten tons per centimeter of length, and with lengths on the order of galaxies or even more. A single string might stretch across the universe (or at least our own domain of the universe).

And consider the WIMPS. These are suggested Weakly Interacting Massive Particles. Again left over from the Big Bang, they come out of some working models of grand unification theories. By definition they interact very weakly with the rest of the universe (in particular with any instruments designed to detect them), so they have not yet been observed.

Nor have the cosmic strings. The theorists may be completely wrong about their existence, but experiments have been suggested that might observe them,[4] so perhaps with further analysis—and a little bit of luck—we will get the answer and know the future fate of the universe.

4. Because that's what this is all about. In terms of the universe, a mass density less than the critical density would mean that the force of the Big Bang is greater than the total force of gravity, and in this case eventually all the galaxies will fly apart from each other and end up as isolated islands in space. Within each galaxy every star will go through its cycle of nuclear fusions until finally all the possible nuclear fuel is used, and one by one the stars will dim or explode, and go out. The universe will end as hundreds of billions of galaxies, each with hundreds of billions of stars, infinitely far from each other, cold and dead and lifeless.

This is one possible end to the universe. But another possibility is even more interesting.

Suppose the universal mass density is greater than the critical density. Then the universe is closed, and the restoring force of gravity is greater than the destructive force of the Big Bang. Then eventually all the galaxies will slow as gravity brakes them, and then they will stop, and then they will begin to fall toward each other. Eventually they will all slam together and collide. What a cataclysmic explosion that would be! It might be, in fact, equivalent to the Big Bang that started it all. In other words, the universe might restore itself to its original state.

Another way of looking at this is through the Heisenberg Uncertainty Principle, and quantum mechanics.

5. Quantum mechanics is the theory that deals with the smallest particles in the universe. Just as relativity takes over from classical ideas, such as Newton's, when the speed of objects reaches close to that of light, so quantum mechanics takes over when the size of objects gets down toward the atomic level and smaller. And just as the results of relativity seem so weird to us, so, too, are the results of quantum theory—and of them all, none is weirder than the uncertainty principle.

Werner Heisenberg was a German scientist in the early years of this

[4]A short but interesting article about one of these experiments can be found in the *New Yorker*, July 13, 1987, p. 13.

century, one of the founders of quantum mechanics. A basic principle of that theory is his famous statement about the uncertainty inherent in the universe, which limits the application of all other universal laws in the same way that diplomatic privilege limits the application of national laws. In the city of Washington, D.C., for example, the law says you may not do certain things, but if those things are done within the confines of a foreign diplomatic mission, the laws do not apply.

In its most usual form, the uncertainty principle says that it is impossible to determine both the position and the direction of motion of a particle with precise exactitude. Mathematically it is written as

$$\Delta x \cdot \Delta p_x > \hbar$$

which says that the uncertainty in position (Δx) times the uncertainty in momentum in the x-direction (Δp_x) must be greater than some finite value ($\hbar$, pronounced h-bar), given roughly by h, which is a constant called Planck's constant (h) divided by 2π. Another form of this principle is

$$\Delta E \cdot \Delta t > \hbar$$

which says that the uncertainty in energy times the uncertainty in time must be greater than $\hbar$.

But if quantum mechanics, as I said, refers only to the smallest things—subatomic particles—what does it have to do with the structure of the largest thing in the universe: the universe itself?

Suppose that the force of gravity is sufficient for the universe to restore itself to its original state. Then everything is as it was before, nothing has changed, and so the total energy expended during the lifetime of the universe is zero. Then the uncertainty must be zero. And if this is so, then the spread (uncertainty) in its lifetime could be any amount at all, even an amount as large as many billions of years.

And the point of the uncertainty principle is that nothing is determined, or restricted, within the allowed uncertainties—which means that anything is allowed! The basic laws, such as conservation of mass and energy, for example, can be violated with impunity *if they occur only within the limits of the uncertainty principle,* just as the laws of the city of

Washington can be violated within the limits of a foreign diplomatic mission.

To be precise, the law that says matter can not be created out of nothing is actually no restriction at all to the creation of matter—if the created matter disappears again within the time limits of Heisenberg's principle. In such a case there would be no violation of the law outside of the boundaries of the principle, and inside it anything can happen.

The universe itself, then, could spring into existence out of nothing so long as it disappears again before the time-spread allowed by uncertainty runs out. We might call this the Cinderella Universe, with midnight striking at the limit of uncertainty.

In effect, if this is true, the universe doesn't really exist—except, of course, within the bounds of the uncertainty principle. It springs out of nothing, and as midnight strikes, it returns to nothing, and all then is as it was before. The laws of physics are not broken by this, since within the limits of uncertainty nothing is known, and beyond those limits the universe doesn't exist.

If this is true, you can see that the real universe is simply nothing. Nothing in reality exists, but as time unfolds, fluctuations in this nothingness can arise because of Heisenberg. Mass and energy can simply spring into being, as long as they will someday disappear from being again, within the time constraints allowed by the principle.

This would allow an infinite succession of universes coming into being and disappearing again. In physical terms this would mean a universe would come into being with a Big Bang and would expand for billions of years. During this time stars and then planets would form, and on some of those planets life would form, and some of that life would evolve into intelligent, conscious beings. Eventually the universe would reach the limit of its expansion and would begin to contract. Life would go on as usual for another 10 billion years or so, until the galaxies would begin to collide and everything would fall together in a Big Crunch and disappear back into nothingness. And then another Big Bang might begin it all over again.

Each one of these universes would have no history connecting it to the previous universe. They are totally separate fluctuations of nothingness, in the ultimate sense of reality. This might well be the true meaning of our universe: "a tale told by an idiot, full of sound and fury, signifying nothing."

164

TWENTY-EIGHT
The Future World

I. OTHER UNIVERSES MAY EXIST IN OTHER WAYS. Aside from an infinity of Cinderella universes expanding out of nothing and returning to nothing, each of which might be unimaginably different from our own, we also have the different domains of our own universe, which may have been created at the moment of the Big Bang. Each of these is, to all intents and purposes, a separate universe. They may be separate not only in the sense of space but also in the sense of basic principles, dimensionality, and the laws of physics.

Why then, with such an infinitude of universes available, do we happen to live in this particular one, which is so well suited to our needs?

The answer to this question, as to so many, lies in the phrasing of the question itself. If you look upon this universe as being one of an infinite number of possibilities, the probability of our occupying it seems infinitely small. But looked at in another way, it is not surprising at all.

This universe is, in fact, the only universe in which we could possibly exist, and so the fact that we are here defines this universe as ours. If, for example, another universe of different dimensionality existed, we have seen that there would be no planets in stable orbits possible. Therefore, there would be no domain suitable for life, and so we would not exist. Such universes may in fact exist, but we cannot know about them since we cannot exist in them.

There are many other possibilities, and they all lead to the same conclusion. Suppose, for example, that the physical constants were different in another universe.

Newton's description of gravity is $F = GmM/d^2$. The constant G is the *gravitational constant* and determines the strength of the gravitational field in our universe. Suppose this constant were a little bigger than it actually is. If this were so, then the force of gravity would be greater and stars as they formed would pull their constituent atoms in with greater force. The nuclear fires at their center would therefore burn more fiercely, and stars would rush through their lifetimes more quickly. But if stars lasted for only 1 or 2 billion years, instead of 5 or 10, there would not be enough time for intelligent life to evolve on the planets surrounding them. And so in this universe, too, we could not exist.

If the gravitational constant were a little bit smaller, it would not provide enough force to push the hydrogen atoms together past their repulsive electromagnetic force, and so it would not be possible to form the heavy, complicated elements necessary for the formation of earthlike planets and life. And so again in this universe we could not exist.

Does this mean that someone has directed the gravitational constant to have precisely the value that is necessary for our existence? Or does it instead mean that many universes have existed and will exist, with many different values for the constant, and we exist in this one precisely because it is the one that allows us to exist? The answer to this question comes from Occam's Razor, but each one of us has to decide that answer for himself: Which is the simpler possibility, an infinity of universes without gods, or just one universe created and overseen by some infinitely complex creator?

2. Finally, let us try to imagine planets that have not only suitable elements for life but also suitable orbits around a suitable star. We tend to think that life will eventually form on such planets, but what resemblance will such life have to us?

This is a question impossible to answer at the present time. Science, after all, is based on observation and testability, and in this case we have only one set of circumstances to examine: our own. In order to determine how life might evolve on other planets, we must have access to at least some limited subset of such planets and see what actually happened there. Then we might begin to form theories to explain our observations and extrapolate those theories to include other possible types of planets and forms of life. But in the absence of such observations our theories are little more than speculation, which amounts in the end to little more than blind guessing.

Perhaps it is even possible for such things as intelligence without life to exist, in the sense that intelligence might consist of a pure energy form with no material body at all. Such speculation is fun but has no place in science until we can make some kind of relevant observation. At the present time we are far from being able to do anything of the kind. But science is progressing so rapidly that it is impossible today to envisage what we may discover tomorrow. With any luck at all the future years will be as exciting scientifically as the recent past, which saw the totally unforeseen discoveries of relativity and quantum theory, radioactivity and penicillin, airplanes and spaceships and X rays and computers and protons and electrons and quarks and neutrinos.

The universe of human knowledge has exploded into unexpected dimensionalities with a Big Bang of its own. Who knows what may be discovered in your lifetime? Who knows if perhaps you will be the one to discover it?

I envy you.

Suggestions for Further Reading

The books and articles listed here go into the individual specialized topics more deeply than this book does. They are a good way to learn more about each of these subjects.

Origin of the Universe

Gribbin, John. *In Search of the Big Bang*, Bantam, 1986. A well-written discussion of quantum mechanics and cosmology.

Structure of the Universe

Albrecht, A., Brandenberger R., and Turok, N. "Cosmic Strings and Cosmic Structure," *New Scientist*, April 16, 1987. *New Scientist* is a British publication, similar to *Scientific American* but more interesting. It is generally available in this country at classy newsstands or in university libraries.

Taubes, Gary. "Everything's Now Tied to Strings," *Discover*, November 1986. An article describing the struggle to perfect a Grand Unified Theory in terms of supersymmetry and superstrings. The magazine is devoted to popular expositions of science.

Origin of the Earth

Fisher, David E. *The Birth of the Earth*, Columbia University Press, 1987. A more detailed look at many of the topics raised here.

Origin of Life in the Universe

Fisher, David E. *The Third Experiment*, Atheneum, 1986. Deals with the experiments sent on rockets to Mars to look for extraterrestrial life.

Search for Extraterrestrial Life

Papagiannis, M. D. "Recent Progress and Future Plans on the Search for Extraterrestrial Intelligence," *Nature* 318, 135, 1985. *Nature* is a scientific journal that can be found in any university library.

The Discovery of Pulsars, and How Nobel Prizes Are Awarded:

Wade, Nicolas. "Discovery of Pulsars: A Graduate Student's Story," *Science* 189, 358, 1975. *Science* is another magazine that can be found in any university library.

INDEX

A

B

Buffon, Comte de, 134–35
Burke, Bernard, 57

C

Calculus, 33
Californium, 93
Carbon, 72, 85, 86,
107–8
Carbon dioxide, 117–19
Centrifugal force, 32, 33
Centripetal force, 32, 33
Chamberlin, Thomas
Crowder, 134
Chemistry, organic, 150
Church
and Copernican model of
universe, 14–15
and Galileo, 25–27
Circular motion, 32–33
Circumference, 54
Cobalt, 91
Color
of light, 81–83
and motion of stars, 49–
50
Condensation theory,
134–35, 137–39
vs. wandering star theory,
141
Conservation, 98

Copernicus, Nicolaus, 11,
16–17
model of universe, 12–
15
Cosmic strings, 66–67,
161–62
Crab Nebula, 90, 98–99
Critical density
vs. mass density, 162
vs. measured density,
160
Curie, Marie and Pierre,
131
Curved space, 44–47, 53–
54
Cygnus X-1, 102, 104

D

De Sitter, Willem, 47
Deuterium, 76
Dicke, Robert, 56–58
Dimensionality, 42–
45
Direction of motion
in curved space,
44
Domains, 64, 67
Doppler, C. Johann,
50
Doppler effect, 49

E

Earth, 119
  age of, 127–33
  end of, 93
Echo satellites, 56
Eddington, Arthur, 47
Einstein, Albert
  and general theory of
    relativity, 42–47
  and special theory of
    relativity, 34–41
Electromagnetic field, 61–62
Electromagnetic waves,
  37–38
Electromagnetism, 64,
  76–77
Electron, 65, 66, 71, 72–73,
  78, 80
Elements, 72
Eliot, T. S., 105
Ellipse, 22–23
Elliptical motion, 33n
Energy, and mass, 40–
  41
Eratosthenes, 7
Euclid, 6–7, 43
Eudoxus of Cnidus, 8
Evolution, 106, 151–
  52

F

Faraday, Michael, 61
Fermion, 65–66
Fields, 60–62
Fireball radiation, 56–59
Fluorine, 92
Forces, 60–62, 76–77
Fossils, 106n
Fourth dimension, 43
Friedmann, Alexander, 48
Frost, Robert, 93

G

Galaxies, 50, 60, 104–5
  life elsewhere in, 148–54
Galilean relativity, 36
Galileo Galilei, 25–28
Gamow, George, 52
Gedankenexperiment, 19, 32,
  53, 100
Geometry, 6–7, 43
Giant Red Spot, 122
Gold, Tommy, 97–99
Grand unified theories
  (GUTs), 65

Gravitational constant, 31,
165–66
Gravitational field, 61
Gravitino, 66
Graviton, 65, 66
Gravity, 29–33, 60, 62, 64
  law of, 31
  and nucleosynthesis, 77–78
  and planetary motion, 34–35
  and relativity, 41, 45
Great Red Spot, 122
Greenhouse effect, 117
Guth, Alan, 63

H

Heisenberg, Werner, and
  uncertainty principle,
  162–64
Helios, 81
Helium, 74–79, 81, 108
Hertzsprung-Russell
  diagram, 82–83, 87, 106
Hewish, Anthony, 96, 99
Hooke, Robert, 31n
Hubble, Edwin, 51
Humason, Milton, 51
Hutton, James, 127
Hydrogen, 72, 75, 76–79,
  81, 84, 108
Hydrologic cycle, 129–30

I

Implosion, 89
Inertia, 29–30
Inflation of universe, 73
  theories of, 63–67
Inquisition, 15, 27
Intelligence, 152
Intergalactic dust, 160
Iron, 72, 91, 108
Isotopes, 72, 76

J

Joly, John, 129–30
Jupiter, 25, 34, 108, 115,
  121–22

K

Kant, Immanuel, 134
Kelvin, Lord, 128–29,
  132
Kepler, Johannes, 20–24

L

Laplace, Pierre, 134
Laws, natural, 28–31
Life elsewhere in space,
  148–54
Life force, 150
Light, 37–39
  origins, 80–83
Linde, Andrei, 63
Little Dipper, 7
Low, Frank, 145
Lowell, Percival, 35

M

Magnesium, 86
Magnetism, 61
Mariner spacecraft, 115, 117
Mars, 106, 114, 119–20
  orbit, 21–23
Mass, 31n
  density, 159, 162
  and energy, 40–41
  relativity of, 39–40
Maxwell, James Clerk,
  37–38, 61

McCarthy, Donald, 145
Mercury, 115–17
  motion of, 35–36, 45–46
Meteorites, 121
Michelson, Albert A., 39
Milky Way, 50, 105, 140
Miller, Stanley, 150
Miranda, moon of Uranus,
  123
Moon(s), 114–15, 139
  of Jupiter, 25, 122
  phases, 25
Morley, Edward W., 39
Motion
  vs. acceleration, 18
  circular, 32–33
  in curved space, 44–45
  of heavens, 6
  of light, 38–39
  natural, 6, 9
  of planets, 7–9, 12–13, 33,
    34–35
  and wavelength sound,
    49–50
Moulton, F. R., 134

N

Negatively curved space,
  158–59
Neon, 86, 92

O

P

Q

Quantum mechanics,
162–64
Quark, 65, 66, 72
Quasar, 104

R

Radiation, 73–74
  fireball, 56–59
Radioactive, 72
Radioactive dating, 131–33
Radioactive decay, 92, 131,
  161
Radioactivity, 91
Radio astronomy, 95
Radio storm, 95
Rains, Claude, 101
Rapid neutron-capture
  process, 92
Red giant, 83, 86–87
Redshift, 50, 54
Relativity
  Galilean, 36
  general theory of, 42–
  47

of mass, 39–40
special theory of, 34–
  40
Royal Society, 47
Rutherford, Ernest, Lord,
  71, 131–32

S

Salt, 130
Saturn, 34, 122–23
Scherk, Joel, 66
Schwarz, John, 66
Schwarzchild, Karl,
  100–101
Science, 17
Search for Extraterrestrial
  Intelligence, 153
Selectron, 66
SETI, 153
Shaw, Bernard, 27
Silicon, 86
Simplicity, 9–10
Singularity, 48–49, 52,
  63
Sirius, 4–5
Slipher, Vesto M., 50
Slow neutron-capture
  process, 92
Smith, Bradford, 145
Solar system, 33, 113–26

Sound wavelength, and
  motion, 49–50
Space, and dimensionality,
  42–45
Spectrometer, 81
Squark, 66
Stable, 72
Star
  binary, 102–3
  formation, 135, 152
  light from, 81
  motion, 6; and
  wavelength, 49–50
  neutron, 94, 97–98
  and nucleosynthesis,
  79
  red giants, 83, 86–87
  white dwarfs, 83, 87
Steinhardt, Paul, 63
Strings, cosmic, 66–67,
  161–62
Strong nuclear force, 62
  and nucleosynthesis, 76–
  77
Sun, 107, 108, 113
  eclipse, and testing of
  Einstein's theory, 46–
  47
  motion, 6
Supernova, 87–93, 161
Superstring, 63–68
Superstring theory, 66–
  67
Supersymmetry, 65–66

T

Table salt, 130
Telescope, 25
Terrile, Richard, 145
Testability, 17, 46, 48, 68
Testing of theories, 19–20,
  46–47, 137–42
Thallium, 92
Thermal conductivity, 129
Three-dimensional space, 43
Time
  of Big Bang, 54
  as fourth dimension, 43
Triangle, angles of, 6–7
Triton, moon of Neptune,
  124
Two-dimensional space, 43,
  53

U

Uhuru satellite, 101–2
Uncertainty principle,
  162–64
Universe
  age of, 54, 133

Wöhler, Friedrich, 150
Woolfson, M. M., 136

X

X rays, and black holes, 102–3

Z

Zero curvature, 159
Zero volume, 63
Zinc, 91